George J. Varney

The Story of Patriots' Day

Lexington and Concord, April 19, 1775 - with poems brought out on the first

observation of the anniversary holiday

George J. Varney

The Story of Patriots' Day
Lexington and Concord, April 19, 1775 - with poems brought out on the first observation of the anniversary holiday

ISBN/EAN: 9783337225025

Printed in Europe, USA, Canada, Australia, Japan

Cover: Foto ©Andreas Hilbeck / pixelio.de

More available books at **www.hansebooks.com**

THE STORY

OF

PATRIOTS' DAY

LEXINGTON AND CONCORD
APRIL 19, 1775

WITH POEMS

BROUGHT OUT ON THE FIRST OBSERVATION OF THE ANNIVERSARY, HOLIDAY

AND THE FORMS IN WHICH IT WAS CELEBRATED

BY

GEO. J. VARNEY

BOSTON
LEE AND SHEPARD PUBLISHERS
10 MILK STREET

PREFACE

THE bill abolishing the practice of appointing annually a day of "fasting and prayer," having passed the Massachusetts House of Representatives, received the approving vote of the Senate on March 16, 1894, and was on the same day signed by the governor, Frederic T. Greenhalge. The bill also established the nineteenth day of April as an annual holiday. The latter, therefore, is the legitimate successor of Fast Day, which had come to be observed chiefly by its desecration.

The first proclamation of the new holiday was issued on the eleventh day of April, 1894, and gave it, most appropriately, the name PATRIOTS' DAY. Neither the statute nor the proclamation prescribed any definite form of celebration; consequently, there is ample scope and freedom for the preferences of communities and organizations in its observance. The proclamation was as follows : —

"By an act of the Legislature, duly approved, the nineteenth day of April has been made a legal holiday.

"This is a day rich with historical and significant events which are precious in the eyes of patriots. It may well be called Patriots' Day. On this day, in 1775, at Lexington and Concord, was begun the great war of the Revolution; on this day, in 1783, just eight years afterwards, the cessation of war and the triumph of independence were formally proclaimed; and on this day, in 1861, the first blood was shed in the war for the Union.

"Thus the day is grand with the memories of the mighty struggles which in one instance brought liberty, and in the other union, to the country.

"It is fitting, therefore, that the day should be celebrated as the anniversary of the birth of Liberty and Union.

"Let this day be dedicated, then, to solemn religious and patriotic services, which may adequately express our deep sense of the trials and tribulations of the patriots of the earlier and of the latter days, and also especially our gratitude to Almighty God, who crowned the heroic struggles of the founders and preservers of our country with victory and peace."

It is earnestly and devoutly to be desired that the sentiments of this proclamation shall imbue every breast; that patriotism shall more and more take the form of religion, holding relation, not to one nation only, but to all the peoples of the earth ; that the happy time may come when justice, forbearance, and magnanimity will so prevail among men that violent and destructive differences between individuals, communities, states, and nations will be prevented by wise tribunals chosen and empowered to adjudicate disputes and establish peace and amity in all lands.

For the incidents and data of this presentation of the opening conflict of our Revolutionary War, I am indebted in part to several works, a list of which may be found on the last page of this volume.

The illustrative views, except those of Lexington Green, Paul Revere, and the diagrams of Concord and Lexington, are from photographs made since 1875; and most of the objects remain the same to the present date.

The view of the conflict at Lexington is from a copper-plate engraving made previous to December, 1775, and accurately represents the scene as preserved also by history and tradition. A room in the building at the left (Buckman's Tavern) was used by John Hancock as an office while the Provincial Congress held its sessions in Concord. The large building in the middle is the first church, with the belfry on the ground near by, as it stood at the time. Another illustration in the poems is from a recent photograph of the same belfry as it now appears.

It should be explained that the patriots' guns were not pointed as shown in the picture until the British had opened fire.   In the background appear the ranks of the main body of the "Regulars" on the march towards Concord, nearly seven miles to the right of Lexington Green, or "Common" as it has been called in recent years.

BOSTON, *April* 3, 1895.

CONTENTS

LIST OF ILLUSTRATIONS

INTRODUCTION

THE 19th of April is the most important date in our national calendar; for on this day, A.D. 1775,

> " By the rude bridge that arched the flood,
>   Their flag to April's breeze unfurled,
>   Here once the embattled farmers stood,
>   And fired the shot heard round the world."

The whole world is freer to-day, and the condition of mankind better, for the events of that date. Though the honor and the misfortune of the initiatory conflict of the Revolution occurred in Massachusetts, the war might have begun in any of the thirteen original States (held as colonies by England), for in all there existed the same love of liberty, the same indignation at the subversions and exactions of the king and Parliament, which had been continued, with brief respites, almost ever since immigration began; and in nearly all there had been forcible resistance to the oppressions which had been found most offensive. All had become pioneers in a wild country

1

under charters which gave them the same right of self-government which they had as citizens of England in their own Parliament; or, in those instances where it was really not so, they had come believing that their English rights came with them to the new dominion. Before 1643 they had occasion to protest against the subjection of the English in America to a legislative body located in England; and the Parliament of the Commonwealth, during the Protectorate of Cromwell, had admitted the justice of their position. From first to last, their purpose of free government, such as the mother country has accorded to Canada, never faltered. The General Court of Massachusetts, while evincing its loyalty to the English sovereign, and consenting that America might be expected to contribute something toward the national expenses, yet insisted that taxation without representation was tyranny; and the people in every way placed themselves in opposition to the enforcement of laws in whose making they had no voice. When the climax of the contest came, there were noble Englishmen in Parliament (among whom was William Pitt, Earl of Chatham) who asserted as strongly as themselves the right of the colonists as Englishmen; but the avaricious and tyrannical ma jority was in power; and, in consequence, General Gage was sent over as governor of New England, accompanied by an army and fleet with which to subjugate their own kin. At Massachusetts Bay was the head and front of the offending colonies, and there the heaviest blow was aimed. The British ministry believed that, with Boston under military control, the whole country would be overawed. The result was quite the contrary. Everywhere in the colonies the people showed their sympathy with the Bay colony, and began to make preparations to defend their own rights, when the blow should fall upon them, by special organizations and in other ways, and by instituting closer communication with other patriotic organizations in all parts of the country.

Again, on the 19th of April, 1783, the cessation of hostilities between the United States and England was proclaimed to the army by General Washington; the exchange of ratifications of the preliminary articles of a treaty having been made. The proclamation was read at the head of every regiment and corps of the army; after which the chaplains of the several brigades, in their presence, rendered thanks to Almighty God. · General Washington, in his orders for the day, said, "The commander-in-chief, far from endeavoring to stifle the feelings of joy in his own bosom, offers his most cordial congratulations on the occasion to all the officers of every denomination, to all the troops of the United States in general, and in particular to those gallant and persevering men who had resolved to defend the rights of their invaded country so long as the war should continue. For these are the men who ought to be considered as the pride and boast of the American army; and who, crowned with well-earned laurels, may soon withdraw from the field of glory to the more tranquil walks of civil life."

Well, indeed, would it be for all our States to set apart for chaste observation that day of all in the year marked by the first brave resistance of our ancestors as the birthday of a nation of freemen; and again, after eight years of painful labors and bloody battles, signalized by the proclamation of the noble leader of its armies, that the dreadful conflict had been brought to a successful end, and the independence of the United States established.

THE STORY

OF

PATRIOTS' DAY

April 19, 1775

I

THE CONDITIONS IN MASSACHUSETTS
IN APRIL, 1775

In the spring of 1775 the population of Boston was about seventeen thousand, though the commerce of the city was almost entirely destroyed. The Boston Port Bill, imposed by the British Parliament, went into effect on the 1st of June, 1774, cutting off not only its foreign trade, but the whole of its domestic trade by water. "Did a lighter attempt to land hay from the islands, or a boat to bring in sand from the neighboring hills, or a scow to freight to it lumber or iron, or a float to land sheep, or a farmer to carry marketing over the ferry-boats, the argus-eyed fleet was ready to see it, and prompt to capture or destroy it. Not a raft or a keel was allowed to approach the town with merchandise. Many of the stores, especially those upon Long Wharf, were closed. In a word, Boston had fairly entered on its season of suffering. Did its inhabitants expostulate on the severity with which the law was carried out? The insulting reply

was that to distress them was the very object of
the bill. As though the deeper the iron entered
into the soul, the sooner and more complete would
be the submission. Citizens of competence were re-
duced to want; the ever hard lot of the poor became
harder. To maintain order and preserve life at so
trying a season called for nerve and firmness. Work
was to be provided when there was no demand for
the products of labor, and relief was to be distributed
according to the circumstances of the applicants.
The donation committee sat every day, Sundays ex-
cepted, to distribute the supplies. An arrangement
was made with the selectmen by which a large number were employed to repair and pave the streets,
and hundreds were employed in brick-yards laid out
on the Neck. Manufactories of various kinds were
established; the building of vessels and of houses
and setting up blacksmith shops were among the pro-
jects started."[1] Tents covered its fields, cannon were
planted on its eminences, and troops daily paraded
in its streets. Thus, in addition to the destruction
of its trade, it wore the aspect, and became subject
to the vexations, of a garrisoned place. The daily
cavalry mount of the British in December was three

[1] Frothingham's *Siege of Boston*, p. 37.

hundred and seventy men; and, before the middle of April, General Gage had four thousand men in his command. Fortifications and batteries defended every point liable to attack.

Boston's only connection with the mainland was the Neck, which joined it to Roxbury on the south; and even this, at the period of the Revolution, was divided by a broad creek, spanned by a bridge, which alone saved the township from being an island. On both sides of the creek were strong lines of fortification, guarded by a field officer's guard of one hundred and fifty men. Charlestown Neck was commanded by a floating battery on each side, while the man-of-war Somerset lay in the Charles, commanding the communications between Charlestown and Boston.

During this period the patriots in Boston were making great efforts to send military stores into the country; and, on the 18th of April, the guard at the Neck seized 13,425 musket cartridges and a quantity of bullets. The Committee of Safety and Supplies had deposited large quantities of military stores at Concord, and in March it was rumored that General Gage was determined to destroy them; and as early as the 14th of this month, the committee voted to place a guard over them. On the 15th its clerk was directed to establish a nightly watch, and to arrange for teams to be in readiness to carry them, at the shortest notice, to places of safety. Couriers were engaged in Charlestown, Cambridge, and Roxbury to alarm the neighboring towns; for it had become known that Gage had sent officers out in disguise to make sketches of the roads, and ascertain the state of the towns in respect to political sentiment and military conditions, Concord being one of the places visited. Bodies of troops occasionally marched through the adjacent towns, in part, for intimidation no doubt, but also to exercise them on long marches, to familiarize them with the roads, and to render movements of the troops less significant.

Meantime instructions from the king and Parliament had come to General Gage to take more energetic measures to put down the growing rebellion. There were indications that Boston was to be made a prison, and its citizens held as hostages for the good order of the province, while the leading patriots should be sent to England for trial for alleged political offences. Many people removed from the town, and it was becoming extremely hazardous for those known as patriots to remain. Samuel Adams and John Hancock, who had been attending the Provincial Congress, were persuaded to leave their property and business in the care of others, and to stay out of the city wholly for a while. Accordingly, while the Provincial Congress was in session at Concord, they made their abode with the Rev. Jonas Clark at Lexington.

The General Court, which had been summoned by Governor Gage to meet at Salem on the 5th of October, 1774, was dissolved by him before the day arrived. Its members, pursuant to the course agreed upon, resolved themselves into a Provincial Congress. This body, on the 26th of October, adopted a plan for organizing and maintaining the militia. It also established, as executive authorities, a Committee of Safety and a Committee of Supplies. Committees of correspondence had for months existed in many places under the authority of the towns alone, and now they were provided with a Provincial head. Instructions were given that militia and minute-men should be put in the best posture of defence, and communication was opened with the other New England States in regard to organizing for their common security. This was the situation on the 18th of April, 1775.

.

PAUL REVERE'S RIDE.

II

LEXINGTON'S MIDNIGHT ALARM

[Paul Revere's own Story of His Ride.[1]]

Dear Sir,— Having a little leisure, I wish to fulfil my promise of giving you some facts and anecdotes prior to the battle of Lexington, which I do not remember 'to have seen in any " History of the American Revolution."

In the year 1773 I was employed by the Selectmen of the town of Boston to carry the account of the Destruction of the Tea to New York; and afterwards, 1774, to carry their despatches to New York and Philadelphia for calling a Congress; and afterwards to Congress several times. In the fall of 1774 and winter of 1775, I was one of upwards of thirty, chiefly mechanics, who formed ourselves into a committee

---

1 The original of this document was contributed by Paul Revere to the Massachusetts Historical Society for its collections of 1798. Revere, at the date of his ride, was about forty years of age, and had seen service in the last French and Indian war. He was by trade a coppersmith and brass founder; producing weather-vanes, bells, busts, medallions, etc.; he also showed much ability as a designer and as an engraver on copper. Many creditable examples of his skill in the latter still remain.

for the purpose of watching the movements of the British soldiers, and gaining every intelligence of the movements of the Tories. We held our meetings at the Green Dragon Tavern. We were so careful that our meetings should be kept secret, that every time we met, every person swore upon the Bible that they would not discover any of our transactions, but to Messrs. Hancock, Adams, Doctors Warren, Church, and one or two more.

THE SIGNAL GIVEN.

In the winter, towards the spring, we frequently took turns, two and two, to watch the soldiers, by patrolling the streets all night. The Saturday night preceding the 19th of April, about twelve o'clock at night, the boats belonging to the transports were all launched and carried under the sterns of the men-of-war. (They had been previously hauled up and repaired.) We likewise found that the grenadiers and light infantry were all taken off duty. From these movements we expected something serious was to be transacted. On Tuesday evening, the 18th, it was observed that a number of soldiers were marching towards the bottom of the Common. About ten o'clock Dr. Warren sent in great haste for me, and begged that I would immediately set off for Lexington, where Messrs. Hancock and Adams were, and acquaint them of the movements, and that it was thought they were the objects. When I got to Dr. Warren's house, I found he had sent an express by land to Lexington, — a Mr. William Dawes.

The Sunday before, by desire of Dr. Warren, I had been to Lexington to Messrs. Hancock and Adams, who were at the Rev. Mr. Clark's.[1] I returned at night through Charlestown. There I agreed with a Colonel Conant and some other gentlemen, that if the British went out by water, we would show two lanthorns in the North Church steeple; and if by land, one, as a signal; for we were apprehensive it would be difficult to cross the Charles River, or get over the Boston Neck. I left Dr. Warren, called upon a friend,[2] and desired him to make the signals. I then went home, took my boots and surtout, went to the north part of the town where I had kept a boat; two friends rowed me across Charles River,

---

[1] The house of Rev. Jonas Clark stood on the road to Woburn, about one-fourth of a mile from the main road to Concord, a short distance beyond the meeting-house near which the Lexington fight occurred.

[2] Robert Newman, sexton of the North (Christ) Church. The lights were shown but a few seconds. Surmising that the foe would also see the lights, the sexton hastened home and into bed; and, sure enough, a few minutes after, in came some British soldiers, finding him a very sleepy man.

a little to the eastward where the Somerset man-of-war lay.

It was then young flood, the ship was winding, and the moon was rising.[1] They landed me on the Charlestown side. When I got into town I met Colonel Conant and several others; they said they had seen our signals. I told them what was acting, and went to get me a horse; I got a horse of Deacon Larkin. While the horse was preparing, Richard Devens, Esq., who was one of the Committee of Safety, came to me, and told me that he came down the road from Lexington after sundown that evening; that he met ten British officers, all well mounted and armed, going up the road.

THE RIDE OF ALARM.

I set off upon a very good horse. It was then about eleven o'clock, and very pleasant. After I had passed Charlestown Neck and got nearly opposite where Mark[2] was hung in chains, I saw two men

---

[1] Revere and two companions, in a boat with muffled oars, passed the British man-of-war Somerset within hailing distance, just five minutes before orders were given to stop any one leaving Boston by water. This was at about half-past ten, and the transports were then landing British troops at Lechmere's Point, in East Cambridge.

[2] A murderer who had been executed some years previously.

CLARK HOUSE, LEXINGTON.

on horseback under a tree. When I got near them, I discovered they were British officers. One tried to get ahead of me, and the other to take me. I turned my horse very quick, and galloped towards Charlestown Neck, and then pushed for the Medford road. The one who chased me, endeavoring to cut me off, got into a clay pond, near where the new tavern is now built. I got clear of him, and went through Medford, over the bridge, up to Menotomy.[1] In Medford I awaked the captain of the minute-men; and after that, I alarmed every house, till I got to Lexington.[2]

I found Messrs. Hancock and Adams at the Rev. Mr. Clark's;[3] I told them my errand and inquired

[1] Menotomy was then a part of West Cambridge, east of Arlington Heights. It is now a part of the town of Arlington.

[2] Lexington Green, where the patriots first brought the British to a stand, is about twelve miles north-west of Boston by the road. Concord is six miles west of Lexington.

[3] The time of arrival was a few minutes past midnight. The house was guarded by six of the Lexington militia. Miss Dorothy Quincy, the affianced bride of Mr. Hancock, was also in the house, having followed her patriot lover in his temporary self-exile from Boston.

Revere was stopped by the guard, who, in reply to his demand for admittance, told him that the family had just retired, and had requested that they should not be disturbed by any noise about the house. "Noise!" exclaimed Revere, "you will have noise enough before long. The regulars are coming out." At this statement he was permitted to pass; and on knocking at the door Mr. Clark opened the window and inquired who was there. Revere, without answering the question, said that he wished to see Mr. Hancock. Mr. Clark was wary, and intimated his unwillingness to admit strangers without a knowledge of their business there; when Mr. Hancock (who had retired to rest), overhearing and recognizing Revere's voice, cried out, "Come in, Revere; we are not afraid of you."

for Mr. Dawes; they said he had not been there; I related the story of the two officers, and supposed he must have been stopped, as he ought to have been there before me. After I had been there about half an hour, Mr. Dawes came; we refreshed ourselves, and set off for Concord to secure the stores, &c., there. We were overtaken by a young Dr. Prescot, whom we found to be a high Son of Liberty. I told them of the ten officers that Mr. Devens met, and that it was probable we might be stopped before we got to Concord; for I supposed that after night they divided themselves, and that two of them had fixed themselves in such passages as were most likely to stop any intelligence going to Concord. I likewise mentioned that we had better alarm all the inhabitants till we got to Concord; the young doctor much approved of it, and said he would stop with either of us, for the people between that and Concord knew him, and would give the more credit to what we said.

CAPTURED BY BRITISH SCOUTS.

We had got nearly half-way; Mr. Dawes and the doctor stopped to alarm the people of a house; I was about one hundred yards ahead when I saw two men in nearly the same situation as those officers were, near Charlestown. I called for the doctor and Mr. Dawes to come up; in an instant I was surrounded by four; they had placed themselves in a straight road that inclined each way, they had taken down a pair of bars on the north of the road, and two of them were under a tree in the pasture. The doctor being foremost, he came up, and we tried to get past them; but they being armed with pistols and swords, they forced us into the pasture; — the doctor jumped his horse over a low stone wall, and got to Concord. I observed a wood at a small distance, and made for that. When I got there, out started six officers on horseback, and ordered me to dismount. One of them, who appeared to have the command, examined me; where I came from, and what my name was? I told him. He asked me if I was an express? I answered in the affirmative. He demanded what time I left Boston? I told him; and added that their troops had catched aground in passing the river, and that there would be five hundred Americans there in a short time, for I had alarmed the country all the way up.

He immediately rode towards those who stopped us, when all five of them came down upon a full gallop; one of them, whom I afterward found to be a Major

Mitchell, of the 5th regiment, clapped his pistol to my head, called me by name, and told me he was going to ask me some questions, and if I did not give him true answers, he would blow my brains out. He then asked similar questions to those above. He then ordered me to mount my horse, after searching me for arms. He then ordered them to advance, and lead me in front. When we got to the road, they turned down towards Lexington. When we had got about one mile, the Major rode up to the officer that was leading me, and told him to give me to the Sergeant. As soon as he took me, the Major ordered him, if I attempted to run, or anybody insulted them, to blow my brains out.

THE LEXINGTON FIGHT.

We rode till we got near Lexington meeting-house, when the militia fired a volley of guns, which appeared to alarm them very much. The Major inquired of me how far it was to Cambridge, and if there was any other road ? After some consultation, the Major rode up to the Sergeant, and asked if his horse was tired ? He answered him, he was (he was a Sergeant of Grenadiers, and had a small horse) ; then, said he, take that man's horse. I dismounted, and the Sergeant mounted my horse, when they all rode towards

Lexington meeting-house. I went across the burying-ground, and some pastures, and came to the Rev. Mr. Clark's house, where I found Messrs. Hancock and Adams.

I told them of my treatment, and they concluded to go from that house towards Woburn. I went with them and a Mr. Lowell, who was a clerk to Mr. Hancock. When we got to the house where we intended to stop, Mr. Lowell and myself returned to Mr. Clark's to find what was going on. When we got there, an elderly man came in; he said there were no British troops coming. Mr. Lowell and myself went towards the tavern, when we met a man on full gallop, who told us the troops were coming up the rocks. We afterwards met another, who said they were close by.

Mr. Lowell asked me to go to the tavern with him, to get a trunk of papers belonging to Mr. Hancock. We went up-chamber; and while we were getting the trunk, we saw the British very near, upon a full march. We hurried towards Mr. Clark's house. In our way we passed through the militia. There was about fifty. When we had got about one hundred yards from the meeting-house, the British troops appeared on both sides of the meeting-house. In their front was an officer on horseback. They made a short halt, when I saw and heard a gun fired, which appeared to be a pistol. Then I could distinguish two guns, and then a continued roar of musketry; when we made off with the trunk.

·   ·   ·   ·   ·   ·   ·

PAUL REVERE.

BOSTON, *Jan.* 1, 1798.

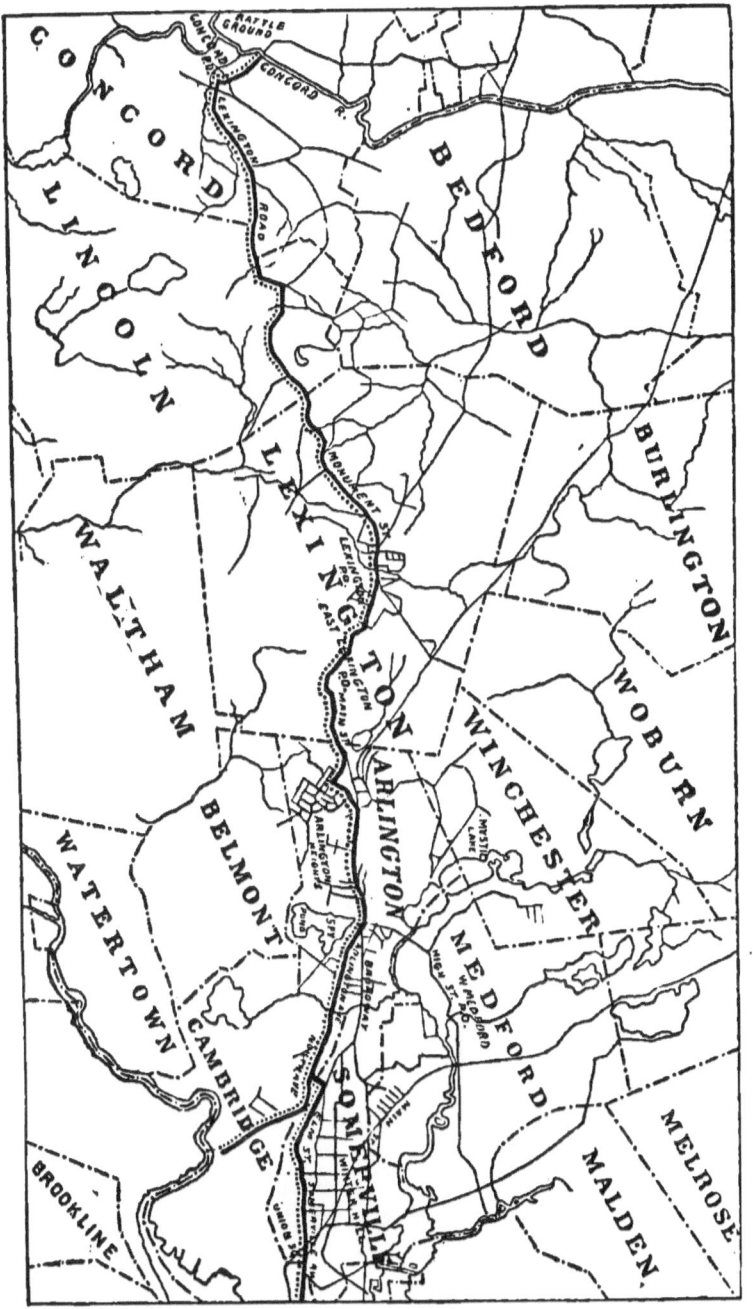

MAP OF BRITISH ROUTE, APRIL 19, 1775.

III

THE MASSACRE AT LEXINGTON

THE two lanterns, hung for a few moments in the tower of Christ Church, at the north end of primitive Boston, showed to the watchers in Charlestown that the expected British raid to destroy the military stores at Concord was in progress. As the moon rose, Paul Revere, the patriot messenger who gave the alarm, was in mid-stream between Boston and Charlestown; and at the same moment the advance of the British, having embarked at the foot of the Common, were landing at Lechmere's Point, East Cambridge. The point is scarcely more than half a mile distant from the place where Revere mounted his horse.

The route of the troops and that which the messenger intended to take joined at North Cambridge; but a couple of British horsemen were already ahead of the messenger, and cut him off from this route, forcing him to take the road to the right, which led through the southern part of Medford. The routes again joined at Arlington Square, between Spy and Mystic ponds ; but Revere had given his alarms in Medford without much delay, and galloped into Arlington and past the critical point a safe distance in advance.

From the landing, the route of the troops lay across Willis Creek to what is now Union Square in Somerville, thence up Elm Street, turning left through Beach Street, past the Davenport tavern into North Avenue, Appleton, Vine, and Main Streets, then through Arlington to Lexington line and along the main road to the Common, where they were first brought to a stand. The force now on the march consisted of about eight hundred infantry, under Lieutenant-Colonel Smith. Before they left Arlington they had caught glimpses of shadowy forms hovering about their flanks, and horsemen galloping ahead of them, and were surprised by the sound of alarm bells and signal guns, and at beacon-fires on the heights ; and, though the usual drum-beat had been suppressed and even conversation prohibited among the men, the commander perceived that the secret was out and the country alarmed. Impressed with the fact, he halted and detached six companies of light infantry and marines under Major Pitcairn, with orders to hasten forward to Concord and secure the two bridges, while he also sent messengers back to Boston asking a re-enforcement.

Major Pitcairn's detachment had not gone far when they met the mounted officers who had captured Revere and Dawes, returning at their best speed with the information that hundreds of men were assembling on the Green in Lexington to oppose the progress of the king's troops. This was an exaggeration; yet the minute-men under Captain John Parker had turned out in full force as early as two o'clock, answering the roll-call to the number of one hundred and thirty. All guns were loaded, and the men remained for some time on parade. Then one of the messengers who had been sent to discover the approach of the regulars, returning, announced that they were nowhere to be seen. As the air was chilly, the company was thereupon dismissed, with instructions to be in readiness to rally on the Green at the sound of the drum.

About half-past four, in the gray light of morning, a scout galloped in with the news that the British were only a mile and a half away. Immediately the drum was beat, signal guns fired, and the bell rang out its alarm. All the militia within reach obeyed the call, and were soon formed in two lines on the northern side of the Green, the farthest from the approaching enemy. A Woburn minute-man, who had come in advance of his company, said that he counted thirty-eight men in the ranks, and also that there were as many more who did not belong to the company, scattered behind walls and buildings, mostly non-combatant lookers-on.

The British were near enough to hear the drum beat to arms; and, regarding this as a challenge, Major Pitcairn halted his force and ordered them to load and prime. Then, doubling their ranks, the regulars marched at quick step, and with a shout, up to the meeting-house[1] on the corner of the Green nearest them. A portion of them here left the road, and filed off in platoons upon the wide area of the Green. The feeble band of minute-men was astonished at the sight of this imposing force, which seemed to them to be twice its real number. The scene has never ceased to be a wonder. There stood the little band of farmers on their own training-field, facing the veteran ranks of the king in splendid uniform and with complete equipment. Some of the farmers had seen service in the last French and Indian wars; but that was a more individual warfare, where each in a large degree waged battle according to his own judgment. The old spirit was

[1] The old meeting-house was taken down in 1793; but several of the other buildings which stood around the Common at the time of the conflict still occupy their old places.

in them still; and their companions in arms of this day shared it with them. Again their homes, their property, personal and communal, and their rights as freemen, were threatened; and they were both patriots and heroes, every one.

Major Pitcairn rode forward at the left of his line. He drew a pistol,[1] and, with threats and oaths, commanded the Americans to lay down their arms and disperse. Fearing that in the excitement of the moment some of his men might discharge their guns too hastily, Captain Parker cried out, "Don't fire unless you are fired on; but if they want a war, let it begin here." And he threatened to shoot any man who attempted to leave his post.

Pitcairn perceived that his orders were not to be obeyed; and hearing the report of a gun[2] near a wall opposite, commanded his men to fire. They hesitated, and he brandished his sword and discharged his pistol; thereat a few in the first platoon fired,

---

[1] Pitcairn's pistols, a very handsome pair, were exhibited at the Lexington Centennial (1875), having been loaned by their owner, the widow of John P. Putnam of Cambridge, N. Y. These pistols have a full and authentic history. Pitcairn's horse had to be abandoned during the retreat; and his equipage, including the pistols, fell into the hands of the Americans. The latter were presented to General Israel Putnam, who wore them through the war.

[2] This is believed to have been an accidental discharge of one of the rickety old flint-locks, which had already served more than one generation. Whatever the fact, it does not appear that any of the regulars were wounded by it.

but without any apparent harm.   He repeated the
order to fire, and the whole line delivered a volley.
Several of the gallant little company fell dead or
wounded; the patriot ranks were broken before they
had fired a shot.   There was no longer a question of
their right to resist the king's troops to the death,

Engraved in 1775.
The British at Lexington.
Reproduced, 1895.

and a volley from the muskets of the minute-men
rang out in reply.[1]

---

[1] In Stiles's diary, under date of Aug. 19, 1775, is this record, giving Pitcairn's
version of the beginning of the fight : " Riding up to them, he ordered them to
disperse; which.they not doing instantly, he turned about to order his troops to
draw out so as to surround and disarm them.   As he turned, he saw a gun in a
peasant's hand, behind a wall, flash in the pan without going off; and instantly,
or very soon, two or three guns went off, by which he found his horse wounded,
and also a man near him wounded.   These guns he did not see, but believing

The die was cast; the war had begun; but with such overwhelming odds that further contest could only end in the slaughter of every American present; and Captain Parker ordered a retreat. Yet there continued a scattering fire from men behind walls and trees, and from some who were unwillingly retreating. Jonas Parker had often said that he never would run from the British. He appears not to have been in the company ranks. It is narrated that he had placed his ammunition in his hat, on the ground between his feet. He was wounded, and dropped down; but raising himself, he fired on the foe; then, resting on his knees, he attempted to load again, when he was pierced by the bayonet of a redcoat.

The halt of the British at this place did not exceed half an hour in duration. Two only of the regulars were wounded. Having fired the first volley,

they could not come from his own people, he doubted not, and so asserted that they came from our people; and that thus they began the attack. The impetuosity of the king's troops was such that a promiscuous, uncommanded, but general, fire took place, which he [Pitcairn] could not prevent, though he struck his staff or sword downwards with all earnestness, as the signal to forbear firing." This seems to be a rather lame statement. It is hardly to be credited that the regulars, accustomed to the strict discipline of the British army, and having for months been under daily drill, should have been so little under the control of their chief officer as to fire a volley or two when they were only ordered to draw out and disarm the Americans. The account, as given in the narrative, is supported by many depositions taken within the summer following.

they were so enveloped by the smoke of their guns
that it was impossible for the patriots to take aim
at any one of them.

Two of the Americans were killed after they had
left the Common, a few of the red-coats having pursued the flying minute-men and others up the Bedford Road.   Altogether seven Americans were killed,
and nine were wounded, almost half the number
who stood their ground on the Common.[1]

> "Were these men true?   We ask not were they brave,—
> Men who their lives thus to their country gave!
>
> .   .   .   .   .   .
>
> When such men fall or put their foes to flight,
> Resisting wrong or battling for the right;
> When they of freedom's army lead the van,
> Or fall as martyrs in the cause of man, —
> Man's heart hath never willingly forgot
> The holy day, the consecrated spot,
> Marked by an act of valor or of faith,
> Or by a nobler deed or noble death."

[1] John Symonds with three others had, on the approach of the British, gone
into the meeting-house for a supply of powder.   They had got two half-casks
from the upper loft into the gallery, when the British reached the Green.   Two
of them, Caleb Harrington and Joseph Comee, resolved at every hazard to escape
from the house and join the company.   Harrington was killed in the attempt at
the west end of the meeting-house; Comee, finding himself cut off from the company, ran, under a shower of balls,—one of which struck him in the arm,—to
the Munroe house [near the church] ; and, passing through the house, made his
escape at the back door.   A third secreted himself in the opposite gallery; while
Symonds loaded and cocked his gun, and, laying down, placed the muzzle upon
the open cask of powder, determined to blow up the British if they should
enter the gallery, choosing to destroy his own life rather than fall into their
hands. — *Hudson's History of Lexington*, p. 180.

Some of the red-coats went into the houses in the vicinity of the Green for a drink; but, with a few exceptions, those who had been engaged in the fight soon re-formed, fired a volley, and gave three huzzas for their victory! Colonel Smith, with the main body of the troops, had come up, and all proceeded to Concord without further interruption. But the Americans, at different times and places that morning, captured seven of the regulars, the first prisoners taken in the Revolutionary War.

IV

THE BATTLE OF CONCORD

CONCORD, in 1775, was the largest town in the colony above tide-water. In its literary, political, and social aspect it was not excelled by any except Boston. The village at the centre then contained a church, a court-house, a jail, a grist-mill, and two or three small factories. A few houses stood mostly in groups along the main road from Boston, being most numerous some half a mile south-east of where it crossed the river. The road enters the town from the south-east along the side of a hill which commences on the right of it, about a mile below the court-house. This hill rises from thirty to fifty feet above the level of the highway, and terminates a little past the north-western angle of the old square. The top of the hill is a plain, and on it stood the liberty-pole. The Concord River (main branch) flows sluggishly in a serpentine course through the town on the north-west side of the village, passing about half a mile from its centre. The old South Bridge was on the road running slightly south of west

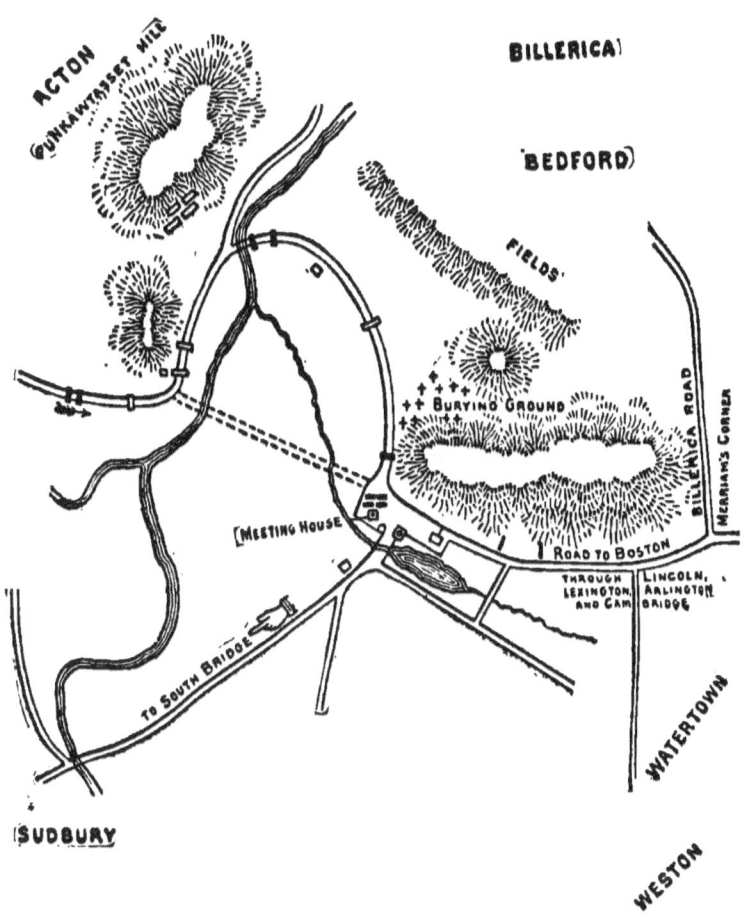

SCENE OF OPERATIONS AT CONCORD.

from the square, while a road running northward and
bending westward crossed the river at the old North
Bridge. From here the road ran in an indirectly
western course to Colonel James Barrett's, about two
miles from the village.

Colonel Barrett had been a member of the General
Court, and was at this time member of the Provincial
Congress. By direction of this body he was in charge
of the military supplies in Concord, a considerable
quantity being stored at his mill and house. He was
also authorized to superintend the movements of the
militia, if called into action.[1]

"It was between one and two o'clock in the morning
when the quiet community of Concord were aroused
from their slumbers by the sound of the church bell.
The Committee of Safety, the military officers, and the
prominent citizens quickly assembled for consultation.
Messengers were despatched toward Lexington for information; the militia and minute-men were formed
in rank on the customary parade ground near the
meeting-house; and the inhabitants, with a portion of
the militia, under the direction of Colonel James Barrett, zealously labored in removing the military stores

1 The organization of the militia was at this time incomplete, both in system
and officers, and without authority from the general government, except partially
in a few cases. "Minute-men" were specially enrolled, to march at a *minute's*
notice.

into the woods and other out-of-the-way places for safety. Meanwhile, their patriotic minister, the Rev. William Emerson, mingled with the people, and gave counsel and comfort to the terrified women and children."

One of the messengers returned with the startling intelligence that the regulars had fired upon the militia at Lexington, and were now on the march to Concord. It was determined to resist them; accordingly, a portion of the force marched off to meet the advancing column. A part of the troops from Lincoln — the minute-men under command of Captain William Smith, and the militia under Captain Samuel Farrar — soon joined the Concord companies. Captains Minot and Nathan Barrett, who had remained at the centre, now led their companies upon the long hill (then called Merriam's Hill) to its eastern end. Scarcely had they taken position when the companies which had been sent down the road returned with the information that the number of the British was triple that of the Americans. Very soon the regulars appeared on the road coming down Brooks's Hill, their arms glistening, and their red coats glowing in the rising sun. Their movement was very rapid; and a line of their infantry filed off towards the hill on

House of Col. James Barrett, Concord.

which the Americans were posted. The militia then fell back to the liberty-pole, opposite the meeting-house. The regulars followed them, but halted when they had come within gunshot. There was little time for deliberation. It is evident that the patriot leaders had hoped to turn the British back by displays of force merely,—not expecting that the number of regulars would be so large. The militia again fell back in order to the burial-ground on a lower eminence westward. They were here joined by Colonel Barrett, the field-officer, who had been attending to the removal of the military stores. He is reported to have addressed them with much feeling, but in a very firm and inspiring manner; and he enjoined them not to fire upon the regulars unless first fired upon by them.

Some were now in favor of resisting the farther advance of the British; while others prudently advised to again fall back, and to delay resistance until other companies should arrive. Approving the latter policy, Colonel Barrett ordered the militia to retire over the North Bridge to Punkatasset Hill, a commanding eminence a short distance north-westward of the bridge, and nearly a mile and a half from Concord centre. As they reached the hill, a column of the enemy was seen

advancing from the village ; and Colonel Barrett galloped off to his residence about a mile south-west of
the bridge, on another road, to hasten the removal
of other military stores. He had barely reached the
hill on his return before the column had crossed the
bridge, and turned along the road towards his house
and mill.

The column of regulars which had followed the
militia along the hill, descended to the square, while
Colonel Smith and Major Pitcairn entered the burial-
ground, and examined with their glasses the position
of the Americans. Very soon the disposition of the
troops was decided upon. The grenadiers,[1] under
the immediate command of Lieutenant-Colonel Smith,
remained at the centre, while a company under Captain Pole was sent to hold the South Bridge,[2] and six

---

[1] Originally, companies who threw hand-grenades ; consequently soldiers of
superior stature, intelligence, and discipline to the light infantry. Their captains were usually mounted ; and the rank and file held themselves as of greater
dignity than other foot-soldiers. In Boston they were often nicknamed
"grannies."

[2] It appears as though orders had been issued to the Sudbury company to
march to Colonel Barrett's to guard the stores there ; and their nearest road was
by way of the South Bridge. But Captain Pole was ahead of them there. In
that company was Deacon Josiah Haynes, eighty years of age. He was urgent
for an attack to be made on the British at the bridge, but the judgment of the
officers was against it. On the retreat of the regulars, he, with the rest of the
company, pursued the regulars with ardor as far as Lexington, where he was
killed by a musket-ball.

companies under Captain Parsons were sent by way of the North Bridge to destroy the stores on the west side of the river. This was the column which came near intercepting Colonel Barrett. About half the force was left under command of Captain Laurie to guard the bridge; while Captain Parsons, with the other companies, proceeded to Barrett's mill to destroy the military supplies in that vicinity.

The British met with but partial success in the work of destruction, in consequence of the removal and concealment of the stores.[1] In the centre of the town the troops broke open about sixty barrels of flour — nearly half of which, however, was saved; knocked off the trunnions of three iron twenty four-pound cannon, threw a few cannon-balls into the mill-pond, and burnt sixteen new carriage-wheels and a few barrels of wooden trenchers and spoons. They cut down the liberty-pole, and set the court-house on fire.[2]

[1] At Colonel Barrett's the British burned a number of carriages for cannon. The officers very politely offered to pay Mrs. Barrett for the food she furnished them; but she refused it, saying, " We are commanded to feed our enemy, if he hunger." They asserted that she should have good treatment, but that they would have to search her house, and destroy all public stores. There were in the garret the small articles belonging with cannon; also musket-balls, flints, cutlasses, and other articles; but Mrs. Barrett had so covered them with quantities of feathers that they were not discovered.

[2] The fire in the court-house was soon quenched, however, by the heroic exertions of the widow Moulton, whose own house stood near by. " While in the village the British seized and abused many persons, aged men who were not

Meanwhile minute-men from the neighboring towns had been arriving at the rendezvous, Punkatasset Hill, until they numbered about four hundred and fifty. They were formed into line by Joseph Hosmer, who, in the emergency, was acting as adjutant. It is impossible to state with accuracy what companies were present at this hour. There were minute and militia men from Carlisle, Chelmsford, Westford, Littleton, and Acton. The minute-men from the latter place were under the command of Captain Isaac Davis, a brave and energetic man.

Most of the operations of the British were in view

armed. Among them was Deacon Thomas Barrett, brother of the Colonel. In his buildings there was a gun-factory carried on by his son, Mr. Samuel Barrett, and men employed by him. The Deacon was a man noted for his piety and goodness, and for his mildness of disposition. Not appearing terrified nor insulting, he began seriously to remonstrate against their violence, and the unkindly treatment of the mother country against her colonies. When they threatened to kill him as a rebel, he calmly said, they would better save themselves the trouble, for he was old and would soon die of himself. Upon which they replied, ' Well, old daddy, you may go in peace.' " — REV. EZRA RIPLEY'S *History of the Fight at Concord*. Another incident was more amusing. As Lieutenant-Colonel Smith, the British commander, was on the point of entering the tavern of Captain Ephraim Jones in Concord village, the proprietor came rushing round the corner of the house to escape some soldiers, looking backward, and struck with much force against the huge body of the officer. (Colonel Smith weighed between two and three hundred pounds, and is said to have been very fat and ungainly.) Both men rolled on the ground together. The officer thought that the collision was intended by the innkeeper, and immediately placed him under arrest. He demanded liquor, — most of which, of course, had been hidden in apprehension of the coming of the regulars. Our innkeeper had the advantage here, and used it ; and not a drop could the officer get until he set his prisoner at liberty.

from the elevated ground of the rendezvous, and fires
they had set were visible in several directions.   The
dislodgement of the regulars from the North Bridge
was under consideration as Captain Davis came up
from an inspection of that vicinity.   Captain William
Smith of Lincoln volunteered to make the attempt
with his company.   " I haven't a man that is afraid to
go," added Captain Davis.   Colonel Barrett then decided on the attack, and selected Major John Buttrick
as leader in this critical movement ; and Lieutenant-
Colonel Robinson volunteered, and accompanied him
as subordinate.   They were ordered to march to the
bridge and pass it, but were not to fire on the king's
troops unless the latter fired upon them.

It was nearly ten o'clock in the morning when the
body of Provincials arrived near the river.   The Acton
company was in front, with Major Buttrick, Lieutenant-
Colonel Robinson, and Captain Davis at their head.
Captains David Brown, Charles Miles, Nathan Barrett,
and William Smith, with their companies, and parts of
other companies, fell into line.   They marched in
double file, and with trailed arms.

The British guard, about one hundred in number,
were on the west side of the river ; but on seeing the
Americans approaching, they crossed to the east side,

formed as if for a fight, and began to take up the
planks of the bridge. The American column was proceeding along a road parallel to the river which ran
into the road across the bridge; and Major Buttrick
shouted to the regulars, remonstrating against the
demolition they were attempting; and he ordered his
men to hasten their advance. When the head of the
column had almost reached the turn, the regulars began
to fire solitary shots toward them. This was the first
firing at Concord.[1] The shots were few in number,
and did no execution; but others followed with double
effect. Luther Blanchard, a fifer in the Acton company, was the first wounded; in a following discharge
Captain Isaac Davis and Abner Hosmer, of the same
company, were killed.

On seeing the British fire take effect, Major Buttrick exclaimed, " Fire, fellow-soldiers! for God's
sake, fire!" The Americans then fired for the first
time, the discharge killing one, and wounding several

---

[1] In regard to the firing at Concord Bridge, the Rev. William Emerson
says: " We received the fire of the enemy in three several and separate discharges
of their pieces, before it was returned by our commanding officer. Captain
James Barrett and several others testified that two of the militia were killed and
several wounded before the fire was returned." Captain Nathan Barrett and
twenty-three other men say that " when we got near the bridge they fired on
our men, first three guns, one after the other, and then a considerable number more: upon which, and not before, we fired upon the regulars, and they
retreated."

of the enemy. The fire continued for a few moments only, when the British retreated in great confusion. They were met by a detachment sent out to support them, but all returned to the centre together.

The Americans followed over the bridge, a portion of them turning to the left and ascending the hill on the east of the main road, while another portion returned to Punkatasset, carrying with them the dead bodies of the gallant Davis and Hosmer. Military order was now discarded. Many had been on duty all the morning, and were hungry and fatigued; and they seized the opportunity to take necessary refreshment.

This was the situation when Captain Parsons, having heard the firing at the bridge, hastened back from Barrett's, repassed the bridge, and saw the bodies of the fallen regulars.[1] It would have been easy for the Americans to cut off this party; but war had not been declared, and, as yet, the leaders were acting on

1 The wounds of one of the redcoats who fell at the bridge gave rise to the charge in General Gage's report of this expedition that the Provincials " scalped the wounded and cut off their ears." The manner in which this soldier came to his death is said to be as follows: A boy employed at the "old manse," which stands near the bridge, came down to the scene of the skirmish after it was over. One of the wounded regulars was sitting up, and while the boy was at the water's edge bending over to dip some water, the redcoat shot at him. He missed the mark, but the act made the boy so angry that he ran and gave the fellow a blow on the head with a hatchet. The manse was at this time occupied by the Rev. William Emerson, who was extremely grieved at the occurrence.

the defensive merely.   Captain Pole, at the South
Bridge, and other small parties not so far away, were
recalled by the sound of the guns to the centre.
Lieutenant-Colonel Smith, having concentrated his
troops and put them in a position of defence, gave
his efforts to procuring conveyances for the wounded.
This was not accomplished, and the retreat begun, until
nearly two hours after the skirmish at the bridge, —
a loss of time that nearly proved fatal to the entire
British force.[1]

[1] The time of the movements of the British troops was nearly as follows:
Departure from Boston, 10.30 P.M. on the 18th (British account); arrival at
Lexington, 4.30 A.M. on the 19th (Gordon); halt of twenty minutes at Lexington (Phinney); arrival at Concord, 7 A.M., "about an hour after sunrise" (Barrett's deposition); skirmish at the bridge, "between nine and ten" (Brown's diary,
in Adams's account, and deposition No. 18, 1775, say "nearly ten"); left Concord at 12 M.; met Percy's brigade at two (British letters); arrived at Charlestown at sunset.

V

THE BRITISH RETREAT

WHILE the events which marked the beginning of a
new nation were transpiring in Lexington and Concord, the news of the hostile march of the British
troops was spreading rapidly through the country;
and scores of communities, animated by the same
patriotic and determined spirit, were sending out their
representatives to the battle-field. The minute-men,
organized and ready for action in numerous towns,
promptly obeyed the summons to parade. Perhaps
they waited, in some instances, to receive a parting
blessing from their minister, or to take leave of weep-
ing friends; but before the British had been driven
from the bridge, all the roads leading to Concord were
thronged by minute-men hurrying to the scene of
action. They carried, in most instances, the old flint-
lock musket that had fought the Indian; with them
was the drum that beat at Louisburg; and they were
led by men who had served under Wolfe at Quebec.
As they drew near the scenes of conflict they learned

that the regulars had been the aggressors in both cases — "had fired first;" and they were deeply stirred by the slaughter of their countrymen. The British had crossed the fatal line; and if any American still counselled forbearance, moderation, peace, his words were thrown away. The assembling bands felt that the hour had come to hurl back the insulting charges on their courage that had been repeated for years, and to make good the solemn words of their public bodies; and they determined to attack the invaders of their soil wherever found.

The return of the regulars to Boston commenced about twelve o'clock. The main body marched in the road, its right being protected by a brook, while the left was covered by a strong flank guard that kept the height of land that borders the Lexington road leading to Merriam's Corner. They soon perceived how thoroughly the country had been alarmed. As one of them wrote, "it seemed that men had dropped from the clouds," so full were the roads and the hills of minute-men.[1] The Provincials left the high grounds

[1] Ensign De Berniere, who had made explorations and diagrams of the towns about Boston, and was the guide of the British on this occasion, says that Captain Laurie was attacked by about "fifteen thousand rebels" at the bridge; and yet "they let Captain Parsons, with his company, return, and never attacked us." This is the wildest of exaggerations. According to numerous depositions taken by the Provincial authorities during the same season, and at least one trust-

MERRIAM'S CORNER, CONCORD.

near the North Bridge and went across the fields and pastures (the "Great Fields") to the Bedford road, which came in from the north-east at Merriam's Corner, a mile or more from the centre. Here they were joined by the Reading minute-men under Major Brooks (afterwards governor) ; and a few minutes later, Colonel William Thompson led up a body of militia from Billerica. Minute-men from other towns also came up in season to fire upon the British as they left Concord.

The Reading company discovered the British flank guard coming over the long hill, and halted in silence some twenty rods short of Merriam's Corner, the regulars having also approached to about the same distance from that point. They marched down the hill with slow and steady step, without music or an audible word. They numbered perhaps a hundred men. Reaching the main road, they passed over a small bridge near the corner, then suddenly faced about and delivered a volley upon the Americans. They overshot, and no one is known to have been hurt. This

worthy British authority, the number was less than five hundred. One British letter of April 30, says: "It was thought there were about six thousand [armed Provincials during the retreat] at first, and at night double that number." Another letter says: "The rebels were monstrous numerous, and surrounded us on every side; when they came up we gave them a smart fire, but they never would engage us properly." This conduct must have seemed grievous in the extreme to the martinet, a character which the grenadiers largely bore.

was not apparent at the moment, however, and the militia returned the fire, two of the regulars falling dead near the brook.

The battle was now reopened, and a severe fire was poured upon the foe from every favorable position. The Sudbury company, under Captain Nathaniel Cudworth, came up in the woods on the south, and attacked them near Hardy's Hill; and there was a severe skirmish on the old road below the Brooks tavern. Here the woods lined both sides of the road where the British had to pass, and a minute-man was behind almost every tree. When the enemy ordered out a flank guard to dislodge them it was merely offering the patriots a better mark. The conflict was short and sharp; and for three or four miles along these woody defiles the regulars suffered fearfully.

The town of Woburn, lying on the north-east of Lexington, had "turned out extraordinary;" sending to the scene of action, with Major Loammi Baldwin, a well-armed force one hundred and eighty strong. They reached Tanner Brook, in Lincoln, ahead of the regulars, and there scattered, firing from the trees and walls; then, moving on, they made repeated attacks from new points. Before the British had re-entered Lexington, Captain Parker's brave company, which had made the first fight on Lexington Green, appeared in the field and did efficient service. "The enemy," said Colonel Baldwin, "marched very fast, and left many dead and wounded, and a few tired." Eight of the dead were buried in the Lincoln graveyard. Of the Americans, Captain Jonathan Wilson of Bedford, Nathaniel Wyman of Billerica, and Daniel Thompson of Woburn, were killed here. At Fiske's Hill, as they entered Lexington, a mounted officer was killed, and Lieutenant-Colonel Smith, the commander, was wounded in the leg.[1]

When within a short distance of Lexington Green, the regulars again suffered severely from the close pursuit and sharp fire of the Provincials. Their ammunition was failing, while their light companies were so fatigued as to be almost unfitted for service, being too much exhausted to send out flankers. The large number of wounded caused great confusion, and many of the troops rather ran than marched. The officers tried in vain to restore discipline. The confusion increased under their efforts, until, placing

---

[1] At the foot of Fiske's Hill occurred a personal contest between a British soldier and James Hayward of Acton. The Briton raised his gun, with the remark, "You are a dead man." — "And so are you," answered Hayward. Both fired; the Briton was killed and Hayward mortally wounded, though he lived until the next day.

themselves in front, they threatened the men with death if they advanced. It was a desperate effort, made under a heavy fire, but it succeeded in partially restoring order.[1]

It was now almost two o'clock in a day of unusual heat ; and the detachment must have soon surrendered had not re-enforcements been at hand. Percy's brigade met the harassed regulars half a mile toward Boston east of the Lexington meeting-house, and received the routed and exhausted column in a hollow square.[2] The re-enforcement consisted of three regiments of infantry and two divisions of marines, with two field-pieces, under Lord Percy. They had left Boston at nine o'clock,[3] marching out through Roxbury to the

[1] It was not far from this point that two or three Provincials behind a pile of rails fired on a splendidly mounted officer, who, in directing the troops, had come near them. The officer instantly fell, or was thrown by a violent move-ment of the horse, which then ran directly toward the Provincials and was cap-tured. It is nearly certain that this officer was Major Pitcairn, who was not wounded, but was thrown, and had his arm broken by the fall.

[2] Letters to England from officers who were with the British troops on this occasion, testify to the critical situation of Lieutenant-Colonel Smith's detach-ment, when met by Percy's brigade, and some admit that he must have surren-dered. A British historian (Stedman) says of the soldiers, " They were so much exhausted with fatigue that they were obliged to lie down for rest on the ground, their tongues hanging out of their mouths, like those of dogs after a chase."

[3] The British *Conduct of the American War* makes the following statement regarding the delay of this re-enforcement : " Lieutenant-Colonel Smith's party would have been destroyed had not Lord Percy joined him, and even he was almost too late from two stupid blunders we committed. The general ordered the first brigade under arms at four in the morning ; these orders, the evening

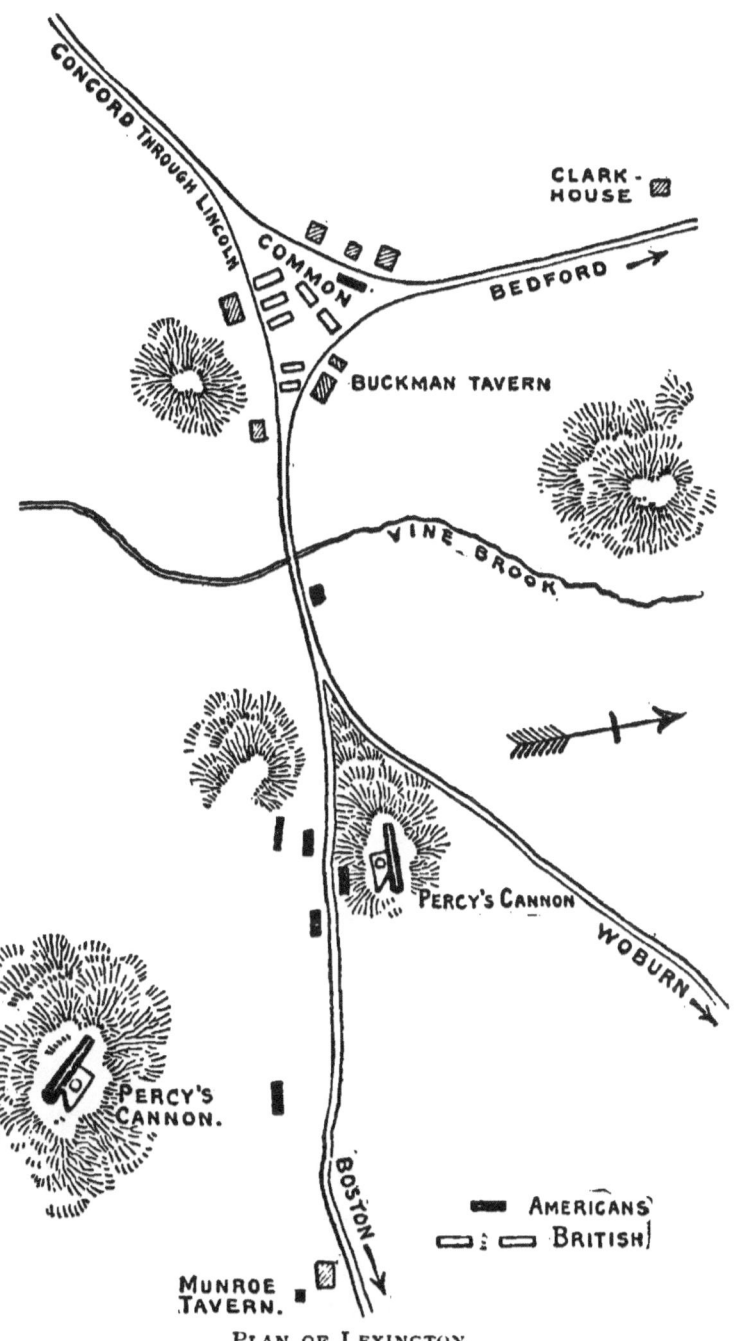

CONCORD Through LINCOLN

CLARK-HOUSE

COMMON

BEDFORD →

BUCKMAN TAVERN

VINE-BROOK

PERCY'S CANNON

WOBURN

PERCY'S CANNON.

BOSTON →

MUNROE TAVERN.

▬ AMERICANS
◻⋮◻ BRITISH

PLAN OF LEXINGTON.

tune of "Yankee Doodle." Their course lay over the Charles River by the old bridge, nearly opposite Harvard College. To impede their march the selectmen of Cambridge had ordered the planks removed from the bridge. This was done; but, instead of being carried away, the planks were piled beside the road near by. The troops soon had them mostly in place, and the column passed without much delay. The provision teams were, however, so long detained that they lost the protection of the main body, and were captured by the Americans at West Cambridge.[1]

before, were carried to the brigade major's; he was not at home; the orders were left; no inquiry was made after him; he came home late; his servant forgot to tell him there was a letter on his table. Four o'clock came, no brigade appeared; at five o'clock an express from Smith, desiring a re-enforcement, produced an inquiry; the above discovery was made; at six o'clock part of the brigade got on the parade; there they waited, expecting the marines; at seven, no marines appearing, another inquiry commenced; they said they had received no orders; it was asserted they had; in the altercation it came out that the order had been addressed to Major Pitcairn, who commanded the marines, and left at his quarters, though the gentlemen concerned in this business ought to have remembered that Pitcairn had been despatched the evening before with the grenadiers and light infantry under Lieutenant-Colonel Smith. This double mistake lost us from four till nine o'clock, the time we marched off to support Colonel Smith."

[1] Later in the day the "home guard" in Watertown showed its strength and prowess. In this town was the home of Lydia Warren Barnard, a woman noted in the town for her strength and determination. Her husband was out as a minute-man, — the able-bodied men, it is stated, had all gone. Sometime in the afternoon several neighbors of her own sex came running to her house, and calling, "Mrs. Barnard! there's a redcoat coming!" Running out she saw, halted amidst a group of women and old men, a British soldier on horseback, who was inquiring his way to Boston. He claimed to be wounded, but in the absence of

Percy had brought two field-pieces, one of which was immediately mounted on the high ground in the angle made with the route by the Woburn road, while the other was placed on another eminence near the rear of his column, on the opposite side of the road ; the Munroe tavern, used temporarily by the British as a hospital, was a little farther back on the same side. These guns kept the Americans in check for about half an hour, which afforded the British force time for rest and refreshments. Though the regulars numbered about eighteen hundred, of undoubted bravery and veteran discipline, Percy made no attempt to turn upon his assailants to make good the boastful insults of his military associates.[1]

sufficient evidence, they took him, rather, for a messenger. Excited and anxious in regard to their husbands, fathers, and sons, the group were ready themselves to do battle against the enemy. The sight of this redcoat "stirred her Warren blood" to action. Striding through the group, she grasped the bridle and ordered the soldier to dismount. As he disregarded her command, she pulled him to earth in a moment. "You villain!" she exclaimed, shaking him vigorously; "how do I know but what you have been killing some of my folks?" He protested that he had not fired a shot. "Let me see your cartridge-box!" She examined it, and found several places empty. At this she shook him still more violently ; and, her anger increasing, she grasped his weapons in such a threatening manner that his fears overcame his courage, and he fell upon his knees and begged for his life. She let him get up, and placed him in charge of the men who had been attracted to the scene. He was subsequently exchanged. The horse he rode was a splendid animal, and his owner was found to be a Cambridge man. The steed had been ridden out by a patriot to give the alarm, and was captured by the British.

[1] Lord Percy afterwards said that he never saw anything equal to the intrepidity of the New England minute-men. — *Remembrances*, vol. i., iii.

THE MUNROE TAVERN, LEXINGTON.

The Provincials continued to harass them as they toiled over the Heights and between the ponds in Menotomy, or West Cambridge, now Arlington. Here the skirmishing again became sharp and bloody, and the troops increased their atrocities.[1]

The Danvers company, marching in advance of the Essex regiment, had taken position to attack the enemy, some behind trees on the side of the hill, others in a walled enclosure, further protecting themselves by erecting a breastwork of bunches of shingles. The British passed in solid column on their right, while a large flank guard came up on their left. They were thus surrounded, and many were killed and wounded. The British also had many killed or wounded in this vicinity. They entered what is now

---

[1] Jason Russell of this place, an invalid and a non-combatant, was barbarously killed in his own house. Near the foot of the rocks a mother was killed while nursing her infant. Others were driven from their dwellings, and these robbed of whatever attracted the cupidity of the marauders. In Somerville (then forming the western part of Charlestown), a family returning to their deserted house found a red-coated soldier lying dead across the drawer of a bureau which he had been ransacking. The diary of the British Lieutenant John Barker states that from Lexington to Charlestown Neck nearly every house was forcibly entered, and "all that were found in the houses put to death." Under date of April 25, he wrote of the regulars on this retreat, "By their eagerness and inattention they killed many of our own people; and the plundering was shameful." It was, no doubt, Lord Percy's marines who committed these outrages; as the soldiers who had shed the first blood at Lexington and Concord were now too nearly exhausted to attempt anything more than getting back to a place of security.

Elm Street, Somerville, (then West Charlestown) on the run, receiving a hot fire from the minute-men in the woods near by. Lord Percy now planted his two field-pieces on the north-westerly spur of Spring Hill, and cannonaded the coverts for a few minutes; but the regulars were soon in full retreat again, passing hurriedly down Milk Row. Some of the hottest firing of the day from the Americans occurred in the vicinity of Prospect Hill; and here Percy again planted his cannon, but with little effect.[1]

The situation of the regulars was now critical in the extreme. By the orders of Dr. Warren, the planks of the bridge over the Charles had been taken up, this time effectually; but the British, for some reason, took the road to Charlestown Neck. Their field-pieces had lost their terror to the Americans, and they had but few rounds of ammunition left, even for the muskets; while the large number of wounded was a distressing obstruction to their progress. The main body of the

[1] Several Americans were killed in this vicinity by flanking parties of the regulars. On the side of the hill two minute-men were firing on the redcoats from behind a wall, when they were suddenly cut off by a flanking-party. The eldest, James Miller, was urged by his companion to escape, but replied, "I am too old to run;" and he continued firing at the approaching foe until he fell, pierced by thirteen bullets. Near Charlestown Neck a boy was killed by the British; and, on the other hand, an officer of the Sixty-fourth Regiment was captured.

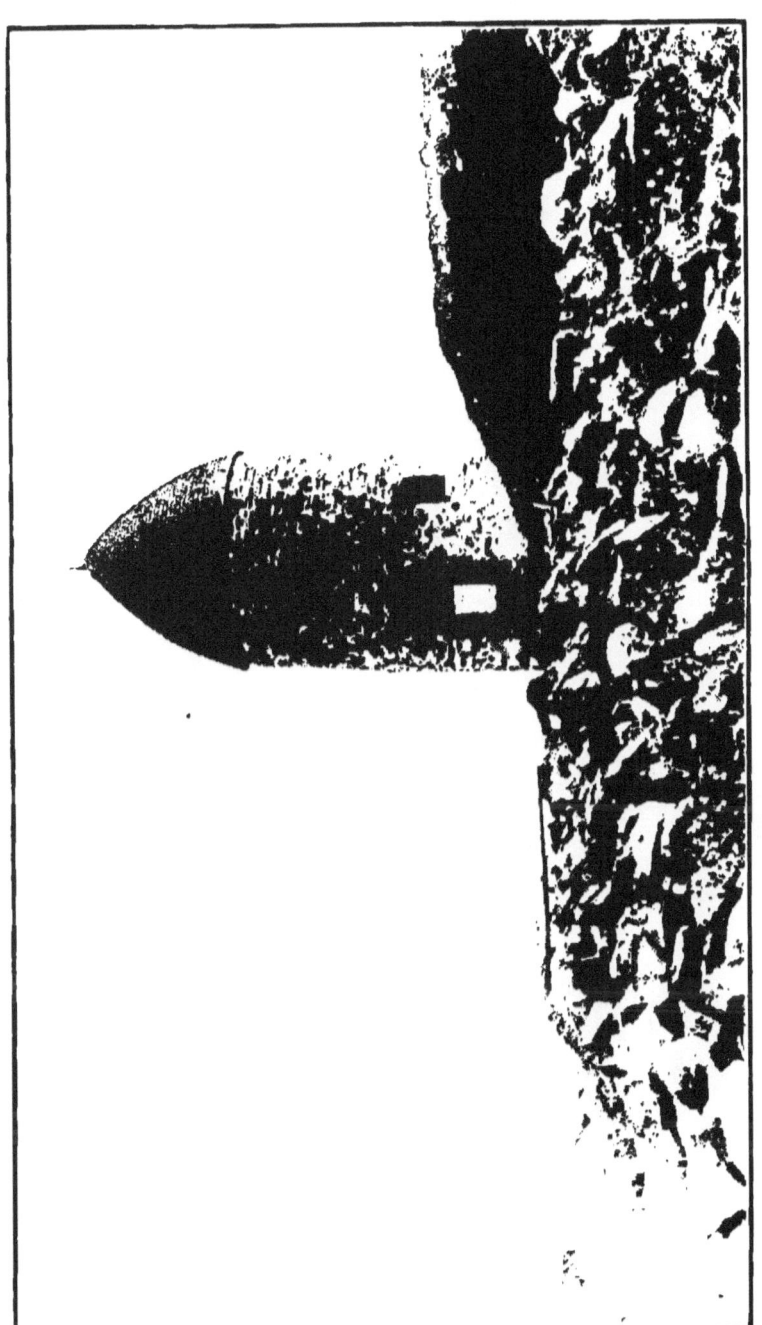

OLD POWDER HOUSE, SOMERVILLE.
(Where, on Sept. 1, 1774, Gen. Gage seized 250 casks of powder.)

Provincials hung closely on their rear ; a strong force was advancing upon them from Roxbury, Dorchester, and Milton ;· and Colonel Pickering, with the Essex militia, seven hundred strong, threatened to cut off their retreat to Charlestown peninsula. General Washington, reviewing this day's work, wrote, "If the retreat had not been as precipitate as it was, — and God knows it could not well have been more so, — the ministerial troops must have surrendered, or been totally cut off."[1]

Charlestown had, since early morning, presented scenes of intense excitement and· confusion, as the occurrences of the day successively became known. Dr. Warren ("General" at the Battle of Bunker Hill),[2] had ridden through the town giving intelligence of the slaughter at Lexington, and a large number of the citizens departed to take a part in the conflict, so that the greater portion of those remaining were women

---

[1] Sparks's *Washington*, vol. ii., p. 407.

[2] It is not to be supposed that Dr. Warren and other patriots were either secluded or idle during the day ; on the contrary, Warren and General Heath of Roxbury were directing the militia during the latter part of the retreat, whenever they could be got at. It is said (I know not on what authority), that, before Percy's arrival, Commander Smith desired to surrender, but could find no officer to whom the proffer might be made. Certainly a white flag would have been respected by every American, and an officer competent to receive the surrender might readily have been found in the truce which a white flag would have instituted.

and children. In the afternoon Hon. James Russell of Charlestown received a warning note from General Gage to the effect that, if a single man more went out armed, "the most disagreeable consequences might be expected."

Many families prepared to leave, and every vehicle was employed to carry away their most valuable effects. Reports had reached them that "the Britons were massacring the women and children." Some remained in the streets, speechless with terror; some ran to the clay-pits back of Breed's Hill, where they passed the night. But the officers directed the women and children to go into their houses and they would be safe; and only required of them to pass out drink to the soldiers.

The main body of the British during the evening occupied Bunker Hill, forming a line fronting the Neck. Additional troops were also sent over from Boston. Guards were stationed in all parts of the town, and everything during the night was quiet. Some of the wounded were carried over immediately, in the boats of the Somerset, to Boston. The next day General Pigot was placed in command in Charlestown, when the troops were all transferred to Boston, and returned to their quarters.

The British loss in the expedition to Concord was seventy-three killed, one hundred and seventy wounded, and twenty-six missing,— the latter being mostly taken prisoners by the Americans. Of this loss eighteen were officers, ten were sergeants, two drummers, and two hundred and forty were privates. The prisoners were treated with great humanity ; and General Gage was notified that his own surgeons, if he desired, might attend those who were wounded.

The American loss was forty-nine killed, thirty-nine wounded, and five missing. A committee of the Provincial Congress estimated the value of the private property destroyed by the British in Lexington to be £1761 15s. 5d. ; in Concord, £274 16s. 7d. ; in Cambridge, £120 28s. 7d. The General Court indemnified all losses.

VI

ON THE BEGINNING OF THE AMERICAN REVOLUTION [1]

THE commencement of the war of the American Revolution — a work worthy of commemoration for ages — cannot be satisfactorily accounted for without taking into view previous effort. Nothing is clearer than that it obeyed the great law of production. It was the result of labor. It took years of deliberation by the people to arrive at the point of forcible resistance; and after this point had been reached, there were months of steady preparation to meet such a crisis worthily. The coming of the crisis, therefore, was not unexpected, nor was it left to stand by itself when it came. The leading patriots were neither rash nor dull, and had both purpose and preparation to seize upon the opportunity and the means it afforded to secure for the country that independence which is proper to a people of intelligent minds and superior regard for moral principles.

---

[1] The basis of a large part of this chapter is the text of Frothingham, in his excellent *History of the Siege of Boston;* but it was found unadapted to the purposes of this volume without considerable modification.

They were men of sound common-sense, who well discerned the signs of the times. If they trusted to the inherent goodness of their cause, they also took care to keep their powder dry.

Many individual volunteers, it is true, appeared on the field on this first day of Revolutionary battles; but the power that was thus successful against a body of British veterans of undoubted bravery, finely officered, disciplined, and equipped, — that twice put them in imminent peril of entire capture,— was not an armed mob, made up of dissociated individuals, who, on a new-born impulse, aroused by the shout of alarm, or the far-off peal of a bell, seized their rusty flint-lock guns and rushed to the battle. No, — it was an organized power, made up of men who had associated themselves, often by written agreements, to meet such an emergency as this; who had been disciplined to meet it, were expected to meet it, and who had been warned that it was close at hand. *They were the* MINUTE–MEN! It is enough to say that they came so nearly up to their own ideal in the performance of a hazardous duty, and to the high expectations of their fellow-patriots, as to win praise from friend and foe. They did a thorough, a necessary, and an immortal work, and they should have the credit of that work. The ar-

duous conflict of the 19th of April, 1775, should be
called *the Battle of the Minute-Men.*

The effect of the news of the commencement of
hostilities, both in the colonies and in Great Britain,
was very marked.

In the colonies the intelligence spread with wonderful rapidity.   In almost every community in New
England, on its reception, the minute-men rushed to
arms.   Hundreds of the muster-rolls, thousands of
individual accounts of the soldiers of the Revolution,
date from "The Lexington Alarm."   Throughout the
English colonies in America the same spirit prevailed.
Nothing could exceed the shock which it gave to the
public mind.   In every quarter the people assembled,
and prepared to join their brethren of Massachusetts
in defence of their liberties.[1]

The Provincial Congress adopted an address " To
the Inhabitants of Great Britain;" and this was sent,
together with a letter, to the colonial agent in London, by Hon. Richard Derby of Salem, arriving in

---

[1] It was the battle of Lexington which elicited, in North Carolina, the Meck-
lenburg Declaration of Independence, which is alluded to in the journals of that
day, and has been reprinted and commented upon at intervals ever since.   The
point of actual forcible resistance had been reached in Massachusetts nine months
previous.   Massachusetts may go even farther back, to the bold Abington re-
solves of 1770, which declared acts of Parliament "a mere nullity,"— producing
a great effect in the colonies.   They were a virtual declaration of independence.
It is said that some other towns were equally bold.

that city on the 29th of May. This address, after brief accounts of the battle of the 19th of April, and of the outrages of the troops, states, that "these marks of ministerial vengeance have not yet detached us from our royal sovereign;" that the colonies were still ready to "defend his person, family, crown, and dignity;" that they would not tamely submit to the persecution and tyranny of this cruel ministry; but appealing to Heaven for the justice of their cause, they were determined to die or be free;[1] and, in closing, said, that in a constitutional connection with the mother country, they hoped soon to be altogether a free and happy people.

[1] In his address at Concord, on the occasion of the new holiday of the 19th of April, Hon. Mellen Chamberlain related an-interview he held fifty-two years before with Capt. Levi Preston, one of the militia-men who participated in the conflict that opened the Revolution. Judge Chamberlain was then about twenty-one years of age, and began his questions to the veteran, he says, with the assurance of one fresh from the school histories. "'Captain Preston, what made you go to the Concord fight?' was the young man's opening question. The old man, bowed with the weight of fourscore years and ten, raised himself upright, and turning to me, said: 'What did I go for?'—'Yes,' I replied. 'My histories all tell me you men of the Revolution took up arms against "intolerable oppression." What was it?'—'Oppression? I didn't feel any that I know of.'—'Were you not oppressed by the Stamp Act?'—'I never saw any stamps, and I always understood that none were ever sold.'—'Well, what about the tea-tax?'—'Tea-tax? I never drank a drop of the stuff: the boys threw it all overboard.'—'But I suppose you had been reading Harrington, Sidney, and Locke about the eternal principles of liberty.'—'I never heard of those men. The only books we had were the Bible, the Catechism, Watts's *Psalms and Hymns*, and the *Almanack*.'—'Well, then, what was the matter, and what did you mean in going to the fight?'—'Young man, what we meant in fighting the British was this: We always had been free, and we meant to be free always.'"

The address was printed and circulated, giving the first intelligence of the battle of Lexington and Con cord to the British public. The news was astounding. The government had information of the state of things in America that was accurate, but refused to give it credit. Speeches were made in Parliament, portraying the consequences of political measures with a foresight and precision that to-day appear wonderful, but the ministry heard them with indifference. It preferred to rely on representations of the colonies made by its adherents there, who were blinded by passion, or swayed by interest; or on language in Parliament dictated by ignorance or pride, which described the great patriot army as a mere faction, and the colonists as cowards, and five thousand regulars as invincible. Hence, they looked to see their imposing military and naval preparations strike fear into "a rude rabble," and produce submission. Such ignorance and expectation were shared in by the British nation. How great, then, was the astonishment to hear that a collection of country people, hastily assembled, had compelled the veterans of England to retreat to their stronghold! The news agitated London to its centre. It engrossed the attention of all classes. It seemed not merely improbable, but incredible.

STORIES

OF

NINETEENTH OF APRIL, 1775

"THE causes which led to hostilities between Great Britan & America are well known to all those acquainted with history. In Oct., 1774, Gen. Gage, having previously ordered the General Court to meet at Salem, & had dissolved or prorogued the court, the greater part of the members met at Salem notwithstanding, and formed themselves into a Provincial Congress and choce Doct. Warren President, and adjourned to Concord, & chose Mr. Hancock, President — they secretely agreed to make preparations to oppose the acts of Parliament, until we should have redress of the grievances we complained of (at that time

---

[1] This story is from the original manuscript of Thaddeus Blood of Concord, describing the ever memorable Concord fight with the British regulars on April 19, 1775, in which he was an active participant. He began as a minute-man, and worked up through the ranks until, in 1779, he became a " Lieut. in Capt. Moses Barnes Company in Lieut.-Col. Perce' Regt., stationed part of the time in R. I. and part in Swansey," as stated in his own quaint phraseology. His account, says the *Boston Journal* (which has investigated the authenticity of this document), is of great value, as he was for many years thereafter a schoolmaster, and so learned to be extremely careful. Therefore, in points where his relation differs from the commonly accepted account of the day, it should not be cast aside as useless. The manuscript was obtained from the estate of Mr. Blood's children by Colonel William Barrett, of Concord.

and near a year after there was nothing said about Independance) — the Congress recommended the forming of companies of minute men, and the collecting of stores & camp equipage; a quantity of stores and cannon, etc., were collected & deposited in Concord, under the superintendence of Col. James Barrett, who had been a member of the General Court for many years, & then a respectable member of the Provincial Congress, and as great a patriot as was then, or perhaps ever, in Concord. He was requested by the Congress to encourage the forming of the companies, to guard the stores and to superintend the movements of the malisha, if called to action, and I heard him several times charge the companies not to fire first as we were marching to the Bridge. By his influence an armory for the manufacture of firearms and manufacture of saltpetre was set up in Concord, and it is my candid opinion that his name should be honorably handed down to posterity. In Feb., 1775, the British attempted to take the cannon at Salem, but were disappointed. From that time there was a guard kept at Concord over the cannon & stores till five or six weeks after Concord fight — here it should be observed that we were all then British subjects, that the officers were nominally appointed over the companies of the Minute-

men, that there was no commission nor any authority
to commission until after Concord fight — except the
malitia officers that were previously appointed by the
King — that all the servises performed were volun-
tary, both of officers & men. On the 19th of April,
1775, about 2 o'clock in the morning, I was called out
of Bed by John Barritt, a Sergt of the malitia compy
to which I belonged (I was 20 years of age the 28th of
May next following). I joined the company under
Capt. Nathan Barrett (afterward Col.) at the old Court
House, about 3 o'clock, and was ordered to go into the
Court House to draw amunition. After the company
had all drawn their amunition we were paraded near
the meeting house, & I should suppose that there was
60 or 70 men in Capt. Barrett's company, for the company commonly consisted of 100 or over, & I think
that about 30 join'd the minute companies or were sent
to guard the cannon that was carried into the woods,
&c., & that the whole of the malitia and minute-men of
the town of Concord under arms that day was not less
than 200, notwithstanding a Rev brother thinks there
were but few of Concord about. About 4 o'clock the
several companys of Concord were joined by two companies from Lincoln, the malitia commanded by Capt.
Perce (afterward Col.), & the minute com'y by Capt.

Wm. Smith — the ven'l and hon'l Saml Hoar of Lincoln was one of his Lieuts — & were then formed, the
minute on the right, & Capt. Barrett's on the left &
marched in order to the end of Meriam's Hill, then so
called, and saw the British troops a coming down
Brook's Hill; the sun was arising and shined on their
arms & they made a noble appearance in their red
coats and glising arms — we retreated in order over
the top of the hill to the liberty pole erected on the
heighth opposite the meeting house & made a halt; the
main Body of the British marched up in the road &
a detachment followed us over the hill & halted in half
gun shot of us, at the pole; we then marched over the
Burying ground to the road, and then over the Bridge
to Hunt's Hill, or Punkataisett, so called at that time,
& were followed by two companies of the British over
the Bridge, one company went up to destroy some
stores at Col. James Barrett's before mentioned, and
they tarried near the Bridge, some of them went to
Capt. David Brown's, some Mr. Ephraim Buttrick's,
where Col. Jonas Buttrick now lives.   About 9 o'clock
we saw a smoke rise at the Court House; it was pro-
posed to march into town, and were joined by Westford
and Acton companies, & were drawn up west of where
Col. Jonas Buttrick now lives.   Col. James Barrett,

THE KEYES HOUSE, CONCORD.
(Opposite battle-ground, showing bullet marks.)

afore mentioned, rode along the line, & having con-
sulted with the officers, &, as was observed, shouted
not to fire first, they began their march. Robinson &
Buttrick led — I say Robinson & Buttrick, for I do not
know what offices they held, but this certain, they had
no commissions till after that time, after Robinson was
appointed Lieut. Col. & Buttrick Major. Upon our
begin'g to march the company of British formed first on
the cosway in platoons, they then retreated over the
Bridge & in retreating took up 3 planks and formed
part in the road & part on each side, our men the same
time marching in very good order, along the road in
double file. At that time an officer rode up and a gun
was fired. I saw where the Ball threw up the water
about the middle of the river, then a second and a
third shot, and the cry of fire, fire, was made from front
to rear. The fire was almost simultaneous with the
cry, and I think it was not more than two minutes, if
so much, till the British run & the fire ceased — part
of our men went over the Bridge & myself among the
rest, & part returned to the ground they had left —
after the fire every one appeared to be his own commander; it was tho't best to go the east part of the Town
& take them as they came back. Each took his own
station, for myself I took my stand south of where Dr.

Minot then lived, and saw the British come from Concord, their right flank in the meadows, their left on the
hill. When near the foot of the hill, Col. Thomeson of
Billerica came up with 3 or 4 hundred men and there
was a heavy fire, but the distance so great that little
injury was done on either side, at least I saw but one
killed, a number of wounded. I know it has been said
that Gen. Bridge commanded the regiment from Chelmsford & Bilerica. He might be some officer in the regiment, but it can be proved that Col. Tomson went with
the regi't to Cambridge and stood till the troops were
organized, and, being old, Bridge was made Colonel.

THAD BLOOD, *serg'ant.*

STORIES

THE only living son of a man who stood in the Concord fight is Luke Smith of Acton. He was the youngest of thirteen children, and thus tells the father's story : —

"Sitting upon my father's knee in the full enjoyment of the blessings of liberty, I received from him this account of the eventful day of history : —

"'The 19th of April, the day of the great battle, was a bright, crisp morning. The sun had been up a full hour and a half. We were drawn up in line when I heard the word of command for which we were anxiously waiting. "March!" How those words still ring in my ears! Luke Blanchard was our fifer, and Francis Barker was the drummer. To the tune of the

---

[1] These narrations were originally contributed to the *Boston Globe* by A. E. Brown, Esq., author of the "History of Bedford," "Legends of Old Bedford," etc.

" White Cockade " we left the town for — we knew not
what end.   We were too much in haste for many parting words.   A few did run back to say a word to wife
or parent.

" ' We took the road for a while, and then left it and
struck through the woods, a shorter cut to Concord.
We passed Barrett's mill before coming to old North
Bridge.   How indignant we were when we first caught
sight of Captain Parsons's detachment of British troops,
with axes, breaking up the gun-carriages, and bringing
out hay and wood, and setting fire to them in the yard.

" ' We had a good mind to fire upon the redcoated
soldiers of King George there and then, but we trusted
our captain and waited for his orders.   When [at the
hill and bridge] I heard him say to Colonel Barrett,
" I have not a man who is afraid to go," my heart beat
faster than the drum of our company ; but how my feelings changed when I saw Isaac Davis fall, and Abner
Hosmer by his side !   I then thought of the widow at
home, whom a few hours before I had seen Isaac so
tenderly leave, after giving her advice as to the care of
the children in case of his death.

" ' But we soon rallied and fought the harder until
the British troops started on the retreat.   I got a
glimpse of Colonel Smith and Major Pitcairn as they

stood with spyglasses in hand overlooking the scene from the old graveyard on the hill.

"'Although we had the great satisfaction of driving off the redcoats, we went sorrowfully back to our homes; for two whom we had loved had perished, and we had the dead bodies as our charge.'"

Mr. Samuel Hartwell of Lincoln, chairman of the selectmen of that town, yet tills the acres which his ancestors cultivated in their small way when they were subjects of King George III.

Mr. Hartwell says: "It was my good fortune to have a grandmother live in the full possession of her faculties until she attained almost a century of life.

"She said, 'Your grandfather left the house with the neighbors as soon as the alarm came by the way of Bedford. They had some agreement as to how the alarm should be spread in case of a movement of the British out this way, and the alarm was sounded here very early in the morning.

"'I did up the chores of the barn, and cared for the children as well as I could in my anxiety. When going out to one of the neighboring houses, I looked down the road, and saw such a sight as I can never forget. The army of the king was coming up in fine order.

Their red coats were brilliant, and their bayonets glistening in the sun made a fine appearance ; but I knew what all that meant, and I felt that I should never see your grandfather again. They passed up the road without molesting me or any of us who were left in our houses.

"'I saw an occasional horseman dashing by, going up and down, but heard nothing more until I saw them coming back in the afternoon all in confusion, wild with rage, and loud with threats. I knew there had been trouble, and that it had not resulted favorably for that retreating army. I heard the musket-shots just below by the old Brooks's Tavern, and trembled, believing that our folks were killed.

"'Some of the rough, angry redcoats rushed up to this house and fired in, but, fortunately for me and the children, the shots went into the garret, and we were safe. How glad I was when they all got by the house, and your grandfather and our folks got home alive !

"'I could not sleep that night, for I knew there were many of the British soldiers lying dead down by the roadside ; but the next morning we were somewhat quieted, and the neighbors hitched up the oxen to the cart and went down and gathered up the dead. I had

got over my ill feelings for the soldiers; and, thinking
of the wives, parents, and children away across the
ocean, who would never again see their loved ones,
I went out, and, leading my little children (your father
one of them), I followed the rude hearse to the grave,
hastily made in the burial-yard.   I remember how
cruel it seemed to put them into one large hole without any coffins.   There was one in a fine uniform, and
I suppose he was an officer.   His hair was tied up in
a cue.' "

Mrs. Herbert Wyman of North Woburn, now of
about fourscore years, had a double share of the narrations of that April day's experiences.   She has
nestled in the arms of two grandfathers who fought
by the rude bridge, and she can tell what many love
to hear.

" My grandfather, Nathaniel Page of Bedford," she
said, " was the flag-bearer of the minute-men of that
town.

" He used to say: 'I had been drilling with the
other folks, and we expected something would come,
but I was surprised when I was aroused at the dead
of night by some one pounding on the house, and cry-
ing, " Up! up! the regulars are coming!"

" 'I got up in a hurry, left your grandmother and the baby, just born, took the old flag that my father had carried years before,[1] and started for Fitch's Tavern, where we gathered according to previous plans. Captain Wilson, who lived down here, was there early; and Thompson Maxwell, his brother-in-law, was with him, although he then lived up in New Hampshire; but he was brave, and would go. When we got together we went in, had some toddy and a lunch of rye bread and cheese, and started. Captain Wilson flourished his old sword, and said, "This is a cold breakfast, but we'll give the redcoats a hot dinner; we'll have every dog of them before night."

" 'We got there ahead of the militia company; but all were in time to help remove the stores to safe places, as we thought. My flag was a bother to me, and I laid it down — not just the thing to do, but we were in a hurry. After getting the stores hid, I came for my flag, and found the boys had it, and were parading about.

" 'We were in the fight at the bridge when the Acton men fell, but we all escaped; yet did not fare as well when we got across the "Great Fields."

. [1] In the French and Indian Wars. See "Flags of the Revolution," in the following article.

" ' We had a hot time, and near Brooks's Tavern came the worst of all. Captain Wilson fell dead, and Job Lane was wounded. We . . . were soon after them to Cambridge, and it proved a great day for the colony.' "

Dr. Thomas B. Hosmer of Bedford repeats the story of Lexington as he had it from his grandfather, John Hosmer, who was with Captain Parker's company of volunteers that morning. Dr. Hosmer, when a boy, went with his grandfather to the field of Lexington, before it was made a park, and had pointed out to him the exact line of the company, and many of the important places to history generally unknown.

His grandfather said: "I stood here when I heard Captain Parker say, 'Stand your ground! Don't fire unless fired upon. But if they mean to have a war, let it begin here.' I saw the British when they marched up in fine order, and heard the command of Major Pitcairn: 'Disperse, ye rebels! lay down your arms and disperse!'

"We were glad when we saw them start on and leave us, but how sad, when we saw so many of our men lay dead, and others wounded, on this field where we are now standing."

Mr. Elijah W. Stearns of Bedford repeats thus his grandfather's story: "I was not in any official capacity when I left home; but after the fight at the old North Bridge, and when pursuing the retreating enemy, my brother-in-law, Captain Jonathan Wilson, was killed, and I took command of the company through the day. We followed on to Cambridge, but I did not stay in camp long. Leaving my son Solomon there, I came home to care for my family. My son remained in camp until he sickened, and he died in the May following."

Mrs. Alfred Mudge of Boston was seen at the Hotel Copley, where she recalled the story reproduced here as told to her by her grandmother, Alice Stearns Abbott, later Mrs. Stephen Lane:—

"I was eleven years of age, and my sisters Rachel and Susannah were older. We all heard the alarm, and were up and ready to help fit out father and brother, who made an early start for Concord. We were set to work making cartridges and assisting mother in cooking for the army. We sent off a large quantity of food for the soldiers, who had left home so early that they had but little breakfast. We were frightened by hearing the noise of guns at Concord;

our home was near the river, and the sound was conducted by the water.

"I suppose it was a dreadful day in our home, and
sad indeed; for our brother, so dearly loved, never came
home."

Edward Reed of Burlington lives in the house which
his father, James, and grandfather, James, owned
and occupied.

"In this room," said Mr. Reed, "the prisoners
captured at Lexington were held in custody.

"My grandfather said: 'I was making ready to
go over to Lexington when I saw some of the minute-
men coming with a squad of the redcoats. They
brought them here to my house, and gave them up
to me, informing me of the affairs at Lexington. I
could not then go on in the pursuit, as I was given
the custody of these prisoners.

"'I did my duty faithfully, treated them well, as
they would say to-day if they could come around; but I
guess they would not want to run the gantlet of the
Yankee again. I had them here in this room (now the
same as one hundred and nineteen years ago). They
behaved well, and I guess they thought they were lucky
to get out of it that way. Fearing their return from

Concord, my redcoated visitors were taken off to Chelmsford, and I was not sorry to be rid of them.'"

Samuel Sewall, a descendant of Chief Justice Sewall of Massachusetts, who, with his father, has served the town of Burlington as clerk a full half-century, tells this story of April 19, as he had it from the illustrious Dorothy Quincy (niece of the "Dorothy Q." of Dr. Holmes's poem), who had become the wife of John Hancock.

Mr. Sewall, then a youth, in company with his father, visited this noted lady, a family connection, at her home, the old Hancock mansion on Beacon Hill; and there her story, given below, came to him, which he has always cherished as a precious memorial of the Dorothy Q. of history: —

"I was a guest with others on the night of April 18, at the Lexington parsonage, being particularly interested in John Hancock, a relative of Mrs. Clark. Samuel Adams was also with us, a guest. I was not a little anxious, for I was aware of the hatred that existed among the leaders of the regulars for both Mr. Adams and Mr. Hancock.

"I was easily awakened when the warning messenger came to the house. I made a hasty toilet,

and was soon ready for the discretion of the officers.
After much reluctance it was decided that we go
over to the parsonage in Woburn precinct, where
were trusted friends of the Lexington minister. We
were driven there in a coach and four, and found a
welcome, — Madame Jones, the widow of the deceased
minister, being the hostess. She was aided by her
daughter and the young minister, Rev. Mr. Marrett,
who later married the daughter of the family.

"Preparations were soon begun for a meal, and no
pains were spared. A fine salmon, given to Mr. Hancock in the morning at Lexington, was sent over to
our stopping-place, and it was prepared for the table.
We were all sitting down to the tempting feast, when
a messenger from Lexington rushed in and told the
story of the carnage there, and that we were hotly
pursued. The coach, a telltale indeed, stood in the
yard. This was secreted by Cuff, the negro slave in
the family; and the male guests were conducted away
through the woods to the home of Amos Wyman in an
obscure corner of Bedford, Burlington, and Billerica.

"There they were forced from the cravings of nature to call for food, which the lady of the house gave
them, such as she had, — cold boiled salt pork, brown
bread, and potatoes, — strange diet for these patriots,

who were in the habit of having the best. But this was the best the house afforded; and the hospitality was in after years rewarded by Mr. Hancock, who gave a cow to the daughter who became Mrs. Seymour."

Mr. Sewall, who recalls Madam Hancock's story, said : —

"We have the very table in the house around which those noted guests were gathered; and it will be spread on the one hundred and nineteenth anniversary of the battle of Lexington and Concord in somewhat the same manner that it was for Hancock, Adams, and Dorothy Q."

Mrs. Pamela Fisk of Arlington is ninety-four years of age, and her stories seem like a new chapter in the history of April 19, 1775.

Mrs. Fisk is a granddaughter of Francis Brown and of Edmund Munroe, both of Lexington, where she was born and spent her early life. Her paternal grandmother was Mary Buckman, who lived at the old Buckman Tavern. So, on all sides, she inherits the blood of true patriots, and has heard the story from their own lips.

"Grandfather Brown," she says, "told me this story :

'I was out here near the meeting-house at the early hour of two o'clock, and answered the roll-call of our company, and in response to the order of Captain Parker, loaded my gun with powder and ball. I heard the discussion as to the safety of Hancock and Adams, then sleeping over at the home of Parson Clark. I went back home and waited until half-past four o'clock, when I heard the alarm guns and the drum beat to arms, and I was again on the Green.

"'The order not to fire unless fired upon deterred me and all of us from having a shot as the British soldiers came up. I participated in the early action, and, having cared for our dead and wounded neighbors, I was in the afternoon attack; when I was wounded by a ball which entered my cheek, passed under my ear, and lodged in the back of my neck, where it remained nearly a year.'" Mrs. Fisk said: "I used to put my finger on these scars, as he told me just how the ball went. We needed no fairy tales in our youth; the real experiences of our own people were more fascinating than all the novels ever written."

Mrs. Sophronia Russell of Arlington, now eighty-seven years of age, in the full possession of all her faculties, says : —

"Some of the delights of my life were the visits to my uncle, Jonathan Harrington, at Lexington. He was the last survivor of the battle of Lexington, living until 1854. By the open fire he and Aunt Sally would sit and tell the story over and over again; for, as the sentiment in the country increased, he was sought out by men from all lands, and became a hero indeed. If Goldsmith had had my uncle in mind he could not have more truly pictured him than he did when writing —

> 'The broken soldier, kindly bade to stay,
> Sat by his fire, and talk'd the night away,
> Wept o'er his wounds, or, tales of sorrow done,
> Shoulder'd his crutch, and show'd how fields were won.'

"My husband's grandfather told me that he returned from the fight to his store, and found that the British soldiers had not only drunk up his rum, but pulled out the taps and let his molasses run all over the floor. Grandmother Russell showed me the route she took when fleeing from the enemy with her babe in her arms.

"She said : 'When we first saw the army coming up the road we were engaged in melting up our pewter dippers and running bullets. So as not to be molested we put out our candle, and were passed by unnoticed by the army, which went up all in good regular order; but such confusion I never saw as they were in when on the retreat. My father escorted me down to Spring Valley (now near the residence of J. T. Trowbridge), and there showed me where the horses of the British, killed in the road, were put, and their bones left to bleach in the sun.'

"The story of the opening of the Revolution has always been a reality in our family. One of the members, Jason Russell, was an invalid and non-combatant, and was barbarously butchered here in his own house when the British were on the retreat. He would not flee, saying, 'An Englishman's house is his castle.' He was shot with two bullets, and eleven bayonet stabs were found in his body." A Bible that belonged to his widow is treasured in this family. In it is written : —

"Purchased with the money given her by some unknown friend in England, in consideration of the loss of her beloved husband, on the 19th of April, 1775, who was inhumanly murdered by the British troops under the command of Gen. Thomas Gage, to the eternal infamy of the British nation."

The Russell family are glad the day is to be known in the future as Patriots' Day.

THE banner here illustrated was carried by Cornet Nathaniel Page in the company of minutemen from Bedford. It is now the property of the town of Bedford. A report on this flag, made to the Massachusetts Historical Society in January, 1886, was as follows: "It was originally designed in England, in 1660–70, for the three-county troops in Massachusetts, and became one of the accepted standards of the organized militia of this State, and as such it was used by the Bedford company." The "three-county troops" consisted of the Colony regiments organized in 1643; of which Middlesex had one, Suffolk one, and Essex and Norfolk together one. This flag[1] is, without doubt, the

---

[1] For the account of the bearing of this flag at Concord, see page 94.

banner carried by the Middlesex regiment from that date, and was the standard of the patriots at the initial conflict of the Revolution. It is, therefore, one of the most valuable relics of the Commonwealth.[1]

[1] The flag borne at the Battle of Bunker Hill had a blue field with a white union, in which was a red cross; and in the upper staff corner a green pine-tree. It has been stated that a flag having a red field, with the same figures, was also carried on that day. The corps led by Dr. Warren, in this battle, carried a Connecticut regimental flag, — one of those described below.

In the spring of 1776, Massachusetts adopted for service on the cruisers fitted out in her ports, a standard of very nearly the design suggested by General Washington, — a white flag with a green pine-tree central, and above it the words, " An Appeal to Heaven." Modifications of this design — with or without a motto — had a red or a blue field, with a white union, and in the latter a green pine-tree.

The Connecticut troops, in 1775, carried banners of a solid color, — a different color for each regiment, — yellow, blue, scarlet, crimson, white, azure, and orange. They bore, on one side, a vine and the motto " *qui transtulit sustinet*," and (later) on the other side the words, " An Appeal to Heaven."

The pine-tree flag divided its popularity in the country with the rattlesnake flag, which also varied in color of field and position of figure.

The earliest standard displayed in the South that was distinctively American, yet not national, was designed by Colonel Moultrie, and raised at Charleston, S.C., in the fall of 1775. It was a large blue flag with a white crescent in the upper corner near the staff. He subsequently added the word " Liberty " in large white letters.

During the siege of Boston a committee (one of whom was Dr. Franklin) was appointed by the Continental Congress to prepare a national standard. The committee visited General Washington at Cambridge, Mass., and conferred with him on the subject; and he, together with the committee, requested a professor of the college in that town and the wife of their host to prepare a design for a national flag. The design adopted was formed of thirteen red and white stripes, placed in alternation, with the "Union Jack" in the upper staff corner, for a union. On Prospect Hill, Somerville (adjoining the Charlestown District of Boston), is a stone erected by a historical society of the city, — a part of the inscription reading as follows : " On this hill the Union Flag, with its thirteen stripes, the emblem of the United Colonies, first bade defiance to an enemy January 1, 1776." A flag of full size of this design was raised on a hill in Cambridge on January 2, 1776, by the hands of General Washington himself.

This design, without doubt, was the one used in the flags made under the direction of Dr. Franklin by Mrs. Betsy Ross of Philadelphia in the following spring. General Washington visited Philadelphia in June, '76-7, and was requested by Congress, together with Hon. Robert Morris and Colonel George Ross, to prepare a national standard. Accordingly they carried to Mrs. Ross a rude design of a flag with thirteen stripes, alternately red and white, the union having thirteen stars in a blue field. There can be little doubt that it was one of the flags made by her from these designs which was displayed in the Hall of Independence, and another flung to the breeze from the cupola of the building, at the close of the prayer offered by the chaplain of Congress immediately after the adoption of the Declaration of Independence.

Congress took no further action in this matter until June 14, 1777, when it adopted a resolve " That the flag of the thirteen United States be thirteen stripes alternate red and white; that the union be thirteen stars, white in a blue field, representing a new constellation."

This flag — with additional stars, as subsequently provided by Congress — has ever since been the standard of the United States of America.

POEMS

BROUGHT OUT BY THE FIRST CELEBRATION

OF

PATRIOTS' DAY

APRIL 19, 1775[1]

[By Rev. S. F. Smith, D. D.]

PRAISE to the brave and true,
Men prompt to dare and do,
    To do or die.
Blazoned on history's page,
Men for their stormy age,
Fearless the fight to wage,
    Scorning to fly,

They with prophetic eye
Saw through the lurid sky
    The goal they sought,
A nation of the free,
A land of liberty,
Stretching from sea to sea,—
    O glorious thought !

---

[1] Written by Dr. Smith, author of the hymn "America," for the celebration of the One Hundred and Nineteenth Anniversary of the Battles of Lexington and Concord by the International Order of the King's Daughters and Sons, and read by him at their entertainment in the People's Church, Boston, on the afternoon of April 19, 1894.

They hailed the coming State,
Patient to toil and wait,
    Suffered and bled.
Death strode o'er hill and plain,
With hunger, cold, and pain ;
Hope rose to sink again
    Till years had fled.

Hail, patriots ! Whose brave hands
Over these free, fair lands
    Their flag unfurled.
Men, by all times admired,
To noble deeds inspired,
By whom the shot was fired
    " Heard round the world."

O, sons of noble sires,
Who, through affection's fires,
    To triumphs rode :
Proud of the deeds they wrought,
With countless blessings fraught,
Cherish the land they bought —
    The gift of God.

BATTLE MONUMENT AT CONCORD.

THE DAWN OF LEXINGTON

[By Clarence H. Bell.]

THE sun s last gleam has died away,
And naught remains to tell of day,
Save that above yon distant hill
A golden tinge doth linger still.

From out the town doth softly come
The rhythmic rattle of the drum ;
And on the ships at anchor fast
The flags are lowered from the mast.

Along the margin of the shore
The twinkling lights shine out once more.
Upon the piers and pebbly strand
The keen-eyed sentries take their stand.

The glistening river flows along,
Its bubbling current, deep and strong ;
Beyond the stream, a gentle rise,
The hills outlined against the skies.

Slow down the slope a horseman rides
To where the verdure meets the tides ;

Dismounting there upon the beach,
He holds his steed in easy reach.

The charger nibbles at the green,
And all the tufts doth quickly glean,
Then strains impatient at the rein
More distant morsels to obtain.

The master, with a fervent clasp,
Retains the bridle in his grasp,
And, standing there with eager eye,
To pierce the gloom doth vainly try.

Alone he stands upon the shore;
A nobler form ne'er manhood wore;
Erect and firm, with iron will,
He keeps his lonely vigil still.

Of wealth is he no favored son;
From dawn to dark his work was done:
New England reared such men as he,
To show the world a nation free.

The watcher stands expectant there,
Though dark the night and chill the air;
One point alone attracts his eye,
'Tis where the steeple rises high.

Upon the breeze faint murmurs float ;
The splashing oars of passing boat,
The rumbling wheels, and now and then
The measured tread of martial men.

Commotion thickens in the air ;
Some movement of the forces there ;
The heavy hand on Boston pressed, —
Will it reach out and crush the rest ?

Amid the blackness of the night
There shines a sudden flash of light ;
A gleaming star, an eye of fire,
The signal from the Old North spire.

When Freedom's picket standing there
Discerned the message in the air,
He quickly reached his saddle seat,
His patriot heart in angry beat.

Across the mead at lightning speed
With gory spur he urged his steed ;
Then up the slope along the crest,
The charger's fiery course was pressed.

The rattling hoof-beats smite the air,
As hour by hour the night doth wear ;

By dusty lane, through wooded glen,
He holds the pace, unseen by men.

At last before a farmhouse door
He reins his weary steed once more,
Then plies the knocker fast and loud,
His arm with frantic strength endowed.

From window high a man looks out,
Dull, drowsy eyes, in fear and doubt,
With trembling hand he shades the light,
" What means this tumult in the night ? "

The eager horseman calls him down,
" Come forth at once and rouse the town,
Give up your sleep, forego your dream,
The British troops have crossed the stream."

These fateful words no sooner said
Than on to other homes he sped.
From house to house the message flew,
And far and wide the country through.

In every home was bustle then,
On every road were eager men ;
One common impulse seized them all,
To face the foe, perhaps to fall.

THE BELFRY ON LEXINGTON GREEN.

When daylight came there could be seen
At Lexington, upon the green,
A little band of heroes true,
With hearts to dare and wills to do.

A varied throng, in homespun clad,
With toil-marked hands and faces sad;
The youth with down upon his chin,
The sire with scanty locks and thin.

Not long to wait; the breaking day
Reveals the British on their way.
In solid front, at beat of drum,
Behold the scarlet legions come.

'Gainst such a host what can they do?
To face the storm, alas, too few.
One scattered volley dins the ear;
The farmer greets the grenadier.

But all in vain their puny might:
The seasoned soldiers, trained to fight,
With gleaming steel and nitred lead
Disperse the band, except the dead.

Upon the grass the heroes lie;
But deeds like these can never die.

The Yankee blood that stains the sod,
Like martyred Abel's, cries to God.

The troops pass on, — in peace no more ;
On every side the sounds of war.
Here, single shots ; there, volleys fly ;
The victors yell, the victims cry.

Each sturdy oak a marksman hides ;
Behind the wall the foeman glides ;
In vain the captains urge their men
Against a surge they cannot stem.

They halt, they pause, reverse for flight ;
Might quails before the cause of right ;
And, hasting back to whence they came,
They leave the country all aflame.

New England's blood at fever height ;
The Yankee's fist in anger tight ;
Oppression's might avails no more,
Though drenched the land in yeoman gore.

O monarch on Great Britain's throne,
No more this land thy rule shall own ;
The nursling now a giant grown,
Hath burst his bonds and stands alone !

THE NINETEENTH OF APRIL.

[*By E. Way Allen.*]

A HUNDRED years ago and more,
A woman stood in a farmhouse door,
Straining her eyes to the distant hill,
With a breaking heart, but lips held still,
Then closed the door, and went to pray —
New England women did, that day.

In the hush of night the message came
By a neighbor's boy, uncouth and plain ;
Yet the unshod feet and freckled face
Were clothed by the words with a noble grace :
"The British are coming !   Arm and meet
At the village green by Concord Street !"

Then rolling outward through the gloom,
The church-bell sent the call of doom,
And ere the gray dawn reached the west,
These farmer heroes stood the test, —
Triumphant souls went up to God,
And martyrs' life-blood stained the sod.

Is this the end?   Can this be all?
Slain by a British musket-ball?
Shall all the fate of all the years,
With all their hopes and all their fears
And deathless rights, sink in the grave
Of men who died those rights to save?

Look down the years: The green corn waves
Over God's Acre, sown with graves,
Though counting few, yet twice the band
Whose dauntless valor won the land.
These are the children, those the sires,
And such blood acts as the need requires.

.   .   .   .

The April day rose sweet and calm,
The robin hymned a morning psalm;
The apple-blossoms, pink and fair,
With springtime fragrance filled the air;
When sudden came a jarring thrill,
And the robin's leaping note was still.

A rumble and thud through the trembling ground,
A rattle of firearms' horrid sound,
Tumult and noise down the startled street,
Gasping, moaning, — wild retreat,

Utter confusion, shameless rout,
Panic-struck soldiers wearied out!

Look quickly! look! and look again!
The British regulars are but men,
And ours are men of sterner stuff,
By toil and hardship rendered tough;
Great thoughts have been their daily food,
And great deeds now but suit their mood.

Lexington heroes head the list,
Lexington homes most men have missed:
Never a child but came through pain,
And the greater the sorrow the greater the gain.
Remember, a nation was born that day!
Was the price, do you think, too great to pay?

"Our lives and homes" was the pledge they said,
" For the truth shall live when we are dead."
Their lives they gave, their homes were burned,—
By the weight of those ashes was destiny turned;
And that ours to-day is the first of lands
Is the royal gift from their rustic hands.

A STORY OF AN APRIL DAY.[1]

[*By a Grand-daughter.*]

I'VE a little story of an April day,
I would like to tell in a simple way:

'Twas one hundred and nineteen years ago —
    That was the time of the "Concord Fight;"
And my story is only a little side-show,
A little story I happen to know,
    An incident of that morning bright.

The British were coming — the British were here;
    The minute-men rallied to meet the foe,
With never a thought of shrinking or fear,
And never a dream that fame was so near,
    As they sallied forth in the morning's glow.

In the shade of the forest, not far away
    (I wish I could tell exactly where),
Some women and children were gathered that day,

---

[1] This is a true incident of the Concord Fight. The "Joseph B." of the poem was Joseph Burrows, whose father, Lieutenant Wm. Burrows, served in the patriot army from April 19, 1775, to the end of the war.

Shuddering to hear the sound of the fray
 Which was borne to their ears on the April air.

Well, one of the boys, just eleven years old,
 Whose name and initial were Joseph B.,
With some other lads, who were equally bold,
Forgetting the dangers of which they were told,
 Wandered away from the sheltering tree.

From their mothers' retreat they wandered away,
 And wandered farther than they were aware
(As boys will sometimes do in their play),
Till they came at length near the old highway,
 While some British soldiers were resting there.

These soldiers seemed friendly and very well bred,
 And gave to the boys a welcome glad,
And one of the officers to Joseph said,
As he patted him kindly on the head,
 "Where is your father, my little lad?"

"He has gone to fight the regulars, sir!"
 Promptly responded Joseph B.
 "Well, you won't fight them, I dare aver,
You'll never fight them, will you, sir?"
 "Yes, when I'm big enough," said he.

The officer smiled and winked to the rest,
    And the boys returned to their rendezvous.
They looked on the matter as a very good jest ;
But their frightened mothers were much distressed,
    When the lads had told them all they knew.

The years rolled on, one, two, three, four ;
    Now was the time for Joseph B.
Fifteen years was "big enough" sure, —
So he shouldered his musket and went to the war ;
    And the years he served were one, two, three.

He had served three years when victory came,
    And then he returned to his home once more,
With only a soldier's modest fame,
And simply his own untarnished name,
    Plain Joseph B., just as before.

This is my story of that April day,
    When the brave-hearted minute-men rose in their
        might ;
And Joseph's grandchildren are old and gray,
But they hold in remembrance this tale of that day,
    This little side-show of the "Concord Fight."

THE SONG OF THE NORTH CHURCH BELLS

[*By Walter J. Phelan.*]

OFT when the Sabbath morning time
  With smile of calm the city greets,
Echo the tones of a tender chime
  Over the maze of sordid streets, —

A gray church tower's sweet-cadenced strain;
  In hearts that know, what chords are stirred
Tumultuous, when in soft refrain
  Those century-mellowed notes are heard!
To them from out that belfry high
Its glorious story fills the sky.

With slender spire against the blue
  Bright sky it stands in simple state;
Yet ne'er may tower the wide world through
  So sweetly sing a song so great.

Above the city and the hills,
  The winding river and the sea,
To varied human joys and ills
  It lends a voiceful sympathy —

127

Prayerful anthem, triumph-swell,
Patriot pæan, hero's knell.

And yet whatever strain may be
    That carillon's, or wild or faint,
One burden 'mid its melody
    Rolls ever from that belfry quaint.

At least to boyish fancies deep
    That trancing tower did conscious seem,
Whose voice the morning stirred to leap
    Ecstatic from its memoried dream,
Till thus from thoughts impression'd long
Suggestion caught the old tower's song:

"In me was born fair Freedom's light,"
    (So keen it starts in tingling pride)
"My twin-star beam one April night
    Flashed fateful meaning o'er the tide.

"It lit a patient watcher's eye,
    It nerved a good steed's quivering frame,
Told ready hearts the hour was nigh, —
    It leaped when tongues of angry flame
The dream of hills and centuries woke
What time that glorious morning broke.

" It glittered where a strange low mound
    Fringed yonder hill with ominous hint,
When 'mid the red coils tightning round
    The rifle-flash met bayonet-glint.

"It glowed, when lo! they found their chief,
    More bold investing watch-fires burned;
While trembling spires scarce knew relief,
    Till wide beneath me, seaward turned,
A vast fleet streamed, and on our shore
The red flag fluttered nevermore.

"My spark along a continent
    Its warning sped to far renown,
And lo! the strife no longer meant
    An empire 'gainst a little town.

"But wide the land its magic power
    To maddening conflagration stirred,
Till rapturous from a distant tower
    Outrang th' irrevocable word!
In myriad hearts' high purpose set
That holy flame is living yet."

So proudly peals each silver tongue,
    Delirious-sweet their accents roll;

They thrill the walls whose thunders rung
  When Otis flash'd his stormy soul.

They reach that doubly sacred fane
  Whose ampler breast swelled bold and free ;
To Adams' tireless soul and brain
  They speak the waves that knew the tea, —
And faint or clear, at the breeze's will,
Float o'er the tide to that storied hill.

          .   .   .   .

BY THE RUDE BRIDGE THAT
ARCHED THE FLOOD,
THEIR FLAG TO APRIL'S
BREEZE UNFURLED,
HERE ONCE THE EMBATTLED
FARMERS STOOD,
AND FIRED THE SHOT HEARD
ROUND THE WORLD.

STATUE OF MINUTE MAN, CONCORD.

THE MINUTE-MAN

[*By Isaac Bassett Choate.*]

BLITHE speeds the plough this warm sweet day of
    spring,
When April's sun has broken winter's reign,
Unclasped the hold frost had on lake and plain;
Swift hurry swallows north on eager wing;
To ploughboy's whistle thrush and bluebird sing.
The brook runs glad, escaped from icy chain
Which tyrant winter forged, but forged in vain;
All fields and woods with songs of freedom ring.
Now halts the plough in furrow, ready hand
Grasps ready musket in defence of right;
The ploughboy is a soldier at command,
His country serving well; before the night
Shall sound of musketry assurance bring
That now hath minute-man succeeded king.

THE BUFF AND THE BLUE

[*By E. Way Allen.*]

GOLDEN buff and a deep, deep blue —
The hearts beneath were stanch and true,
Men that a kingdom could not buy,
Men that would dare and do and die;
These were the sort that led the fight
In the struggle for freedom, God, and right.

The deep, deep blue and the golden buff, —
How can we render them honor enough?
We unfurled the blue in our flag on high,
Where it matches its tint with the blue of the sky;
And we buried the buff beneath the sod,
To rise, fresh-born, in the golden-rod.

Golden buff and the deep, deep blue
O'er us to-day their power renew;
And loyal Yankees everywhere,
On head or shoulder or bosom, wear
A knot of the buff and a knot of the blue,
As the patriot wore them, stanch and true.

PAUL REVERE'S RIDE[1]

[By Rev. S. F. Smith, D. D.]

HANG out the lanterns! Let oppression quail, —
The pen of History shall record the tale;
A feeble taper flashing o'er the sea,
But the first signal light of liberty.

Hang out the lantern! Veiled by friendly night,
A watchful horseman waits to catch the light;
Then warn the sleeping people far and near.
Who is the patriot rider? Paul Revere.

Ride on! Ride on! O valiant horseman! Wake!
Fathers and sons, a stern defence to make.
Armed with brave hands, and hearts resolved to be,
Through Heaven's defence, a nation of the free.

[1] On the eve of April 19, 1894, there was a celebration at Christ Church (the Old North Church), Boston, of the restoration of its chimes, and of the signals from its tower for the messenger to warn Lexington and Concord of the approach of the British troops. At one point Dr. Smith attempted to leave the church, but was captured at the door by his friends, and brought back to the platform, while the people cheered. He was besought to make a speech, but confessed his inability so to do. " But," said he, " I have something which I have written here;" and suiting the action to the word, he drew a roll of manuscript from his pocket. From this he read the following original poem.

The foeman started bravely on his way,
But found the freemen ready for the fray,
Waiting their coming — men who knew no fear,
Prepared for battle — roused by Paul Revere.

High thoughts, strong souls, firm wills then showed
        their power ;
Then independence struck the nation's hour.
The patriots won the day, and Percy's men,
Conquered and broken, sought their camps again.

The feeble lantern in the belfry hung,
With flickering rays over the still waters flung :
A central sun, that never more declines,
Still round the world a radiant signal shines.

Strong men, great hearts, the stirring times required,
With matchless zeal and fervent purpose fired ;
But none more grandly served the cause so dear
Than that brave patriot rider, Paul Revere.

OUR COUNTRY [1]

[*By Julia Ward Howe.*]

On primal rocks she wrote her name;
　　The towns were reared on holy graves;
The golden seed that bore her came
　　Swift-winged with prayer o'er ocean waves.

The Forest bowed his solemn crest,
　　And open flung his sylvan doors;
Fresh rivers led the appointed guests
　　To clasp the wide-embracing shores.

Till fold by fold, the broidered land,
　　To swell her virgin vestments, grew;
While sages, strong in heart and hand,
　　Her virtue's fiery girdle drew.

O exile of the wrath of kings!
　　O pilgrim ark of liberty!
The refuge of divinest things,
　　Their record must abide in thee.

[1] Read at the meeting of the Daughters of the Revolution at the Old South Meeting-house, April 19, 1894.

First in the glories of thy front
　Let the crown jewel, truth, be found ;
Thy right hand fling with generous wont
　Love's happy chain to farthest bound.

Let justice with the faultless scales
　Hold fast the worship of thy sons ;
Thy commerce spread her shining sails
　Where no dark tide of rapine runs.

So link thy ways to those of God,
　So follow firm the heavenly laws,
That stars may greet the warrior-browed,
　And storm-sped angels hail thy cause.

O land — the measure of our prayers,
　Hope of the world in grief and wrong —
On thine the blessing of the year,
　The gift of faith, the crown of song.

OLD NORTH CHURCH

THE SCAR OF LEXINGTON[1]

[*By Hannah F. Gould.*]

WITH cherub smile, the prattling boy
　　Who on the veteran's breast reclines,
Has thrown aside his favorite toy,
　　And round his tender finger twines
Those scattered locks, that with the flight
Of fourscore years are snowy white;
And as a scar arrests his view,
He cries, "Grandpa, what wounded you?"

"My child, 'tis five-and-fifty years
　　This very day, this very hour,
Since from a scene of blood and tears
　　Where valor fell by hostile power,
I saw retire the setting sun
Behind the hills of Lexington;
While pale and lifeless on the plain
My brothers lay, for freedom slain.

---

1 The above poem, written many years ago by Miss H. F. Gould of Newbury-
port, refers to her father, Captain Benjamin Gould, and his little grandson, now
Dr. Benjamin A. Gould, the astronomer.

And ere that fight — the first that spoke
  In thunder to our land — was o'er,
Amid the clouds of fire and smoke,
  I felt my garments wet with gore.
'Tis since that dread and wild affray,
That trying, dark, eventful day,
From this calm April eve so far,
I wear upon my cheek the scar.

When thou to manhood shalt be grown,
  And I am gone in dust to sleep,
May freedom's rights be still thine own,
  And thou and thine in quiet reap
The unblighted product of the toil
In which my blood bedewed the soil;
And while those fruits thou shalt enjoy,
Bethink thee of this scar, my boy.

But should thy country's voice be heard
  To bid her children fly to arms,
Gird on thy grandsire's trusty sword,
  And, undismayed by war's alarms,
Remember, on the battle-field,
I made the hand of God my shield!
And be thou spared, like me, to tell
What bore thee up, while others fell."

THE BUZZ-SAW

[By Paul West.]

A CONFUSION OF BATTLES

IT was very nearly midnight,
   On the streets of Boston town;
Only now and then a person
   Was there walking up and down;
But there came a roving spirit
   From the shades of long ago,
And he scanned the people's faces
   As they passed him to and fro.

"I have ridden," he was musing,
   "Many miles since yesterday,
To get tidings for my people
   Of that awful English fray.
They've been fighting out at Concord,
   And at Lexington the gore
Of the patriots stains the meadows.
   It is war, most bitter war."

It was plain to those who saw him
  That the shade was not *au fait*.
He imagined he was living
  In a long-transpired day.
He was talking of the battles
  That have furnished many a rhyme.
He had no thought of the seasons,
  Of the passing on of time.

Down the street there came a person,
  Clad in "sporty" raiment he,
With a diamond on his bosom —
  "Flash" in his entirety.
"Tell me, tell me," quoth the spirit,
  As approached the stranger near,
"Tell me how the battle goeth.
  We have lost, I greatly fear!

"I have ridden from a distance,
  For my patriot comrades' sake,
To inquire about this battle,
  And return ere day shall break.
Have we won, or have the others
  Stained the greensward with our life?
Tell me, tell me, have we licked them
  In this bloody, bloody strife?"

"Well," the stranger said, "'twas dis way:
   Fust it looked as dough de coon
Didn't have no chance o' winnin',
   But would give out pooty soon.
But he kept on gittin' 'foxy,'
   An' at last de jaw he foun',
An' he knocked de odder silly —
   Did him up in sixteen roun'."

Then the shade's eyes bulged and glittered.
   "Hold," he said. "I do not know
Why you twit me with such stories, —
   Sure they fill me full of woe.
Are you talking of the battle,
   Out at Concord in the night?"
"Naw," the sport said. "I am chirpin'
   Of de Tracey-Wolcott fight!"

CONCORD RIVER

[*By Isador H. Coriat.*]

Upon that rustic bridge I stood,
Where once those brave men shed their blood;
'Twas here that Freedom's seeds were sowed,
Where Concord, lovely Concord, flowed.

The heaven's splendid sanguine hue,
Slow changed into a sapphire blue,
And its reflection dimly showed
Where Concord, mirrored Concord, glowed.

The stars of evening sparkled clear;
The hills, the fields, the roadways drear,
No more with the dying daylight glowed,
Where Concord, silent Concord, flowed.

I thought on those whose souls had fled,
Who rest now with the mighty dead
In their sequestered, dark abode,
Where Concord, slumb'ring Concord, flowed.

CONCORD NORTH BRIDGE.
(Showing Statue of Minute Man.)

I thought upon that happy seer
Who wrote with neither scorn nor fear,
Who dwelt serene in his abode,
Where Concord, holy Concord, flowed.

I thought on him whose charming pen
Had analyzed the souls of men,
And of the Manse, near by the road,
Where Concord, classic Concord, flowed.

Upon that woodland sage I thought,
Who after Nature's secret sought;
Whose life-stream in his plain abode,
Like Concord, placid Concord, flowed.

They all now sleep in heavenly peace
'Neath Sleepy Hollow's moaning trees;
Make Thou, O God, *my* last repose
Quiet as lovely Concord flows.

THE NINETEENTH OF APRIL

[*By Joseph A. Watson.*]

WHAT old North Ender, born below
   The chimes of Christ Church steeple,
But feels within his bosom glow
   The soul of those brave people

Who, farther back than " seventy-six,"
   Were vexed about some taxes,
And put King George in such a fix
   By stirring tea with axes !

A hundred years and more have fled
   Since, on that April morning,
Men, numbered never with the dead,
   Heard Paul Revere's bold warning.

Ah, those true men who shed their blood,
   On heights lived, not in hollows ;
And on the " bridge that arched the flood "
   They fired — you know what follows.

What dearer thing by poets sung —
  Its spirit shines unrusted —
Than the "ole queen's-arm that Gran'ther Young
  Fetched back from Concord busted"?

But though 'tis busted, I aver
  It speaks right on forever:
"Be patriots as your grandsires were!
  Be less than free men never!"

———

LEXINGTON[1]

[By Miriam Lester.]

WE name our heroes in the hush
That follows battle's awful roar,
And count the cost of that great rush
To victory! They deemed no more
Than just, the simple right to shed
Their blood in such a holy cause.

[1] Poem written for the celebration of the One Hundred and Nineteenth Anniversary of the Battle of Lexington, and read before the Daughters of the American Revolution at Kendall Green (Washington, D. C.), April 19, 1894.

Where the unconquered died or bled
We turn, from our safe ground, and pause
To wonder how, in days long gone,
Such power was given to right the wrong!

We deem them worthy of all praise,
The heroes of that battlefield;
And looking backward to those days,
.That meed of praise most gladly yield.
Were they more true to dictates bold
Of honor in that olden time?
Or, when the weight of proof is told,
Rang out the truth in purer chime?
Gave they more freely of life's stream
Than we would do?—than we dare dream?

They did not flinch when in the wage
Of war stern duty's standard waved,
But heart and hand did both engage,
And on each soul was deep engraved
"Country and Home!" fit words to urge
To action more heroic still,
As o'er that ocean's mighty surge
Rang out the watchword of their will!
As onward pressed to Liberty
The men through whom *we* now are free!

In conflict rang their cry of might,
"Ours is the cause that must be won;
God is the helper of the right."
So sped the word at Lexington,
While hurrying from peaceful plough
To war's red-stainèd field they came.
Not theirs 'neath tyranny to bow;
Not theirs a country's death and shame;
But to go on to greater height   .
With wing outspread for purer flight.

Hail, heroes in our country's need,
We bring ye wreaths of laurel-leaves;
We gather of the scattered seed
In full and ripened harvest sheaves.
Yours be it e'er to lift our minds
To realms of higher deed and thought;
Be ours to loose what here but binds
And holds us from the object sought.
Then may we hope, in time, to stand
As stanch and true as that brave band.
To-day, as meet, we hold this page
Of history before the world;
While overhead, undimmed by age,
Our country's flag is all unfurled.

O emblém of sweet Freedom's gift,
Not vainly are thy stars displayed.
To thee our eyes with pride we lift ;
Thy Stars and Stripes our strength have made.
Hail, heroes of brave deeds well done,
Hail, day that gave us Lexington.

SUPPLEMENT

.

CELEBRATIONS

OF THE

FIRST "PATRIOTS' DAY"

1894

THE first proclamation for the new holiday in the good Commonwealth of Massachusetts was issued on the 11th of April, 1894. There was no form of celebration to serve as a precedent in its observance, and the time was short for suitable consideration. The name and purpose of the holiday gave wide scope in the manner of keeping it ; which actually, in different organizations and communities, varied from religious meetings and social and literary gatherings to public balls and private dancing-parties, tennis, golf, cricket, and other games ; races, regattas, fireworks, with band music and bell-ringing, salutes, military parades, and sham fights, — thus ranging in character from that of the time-honored Fast Day, whose place the new holiday has taken, to that of the Fourth of July and the old Muster Day.

Of the nearly four hundred cities and towns in the State, there were many which took little note of the day because of a lack of habit and the absence of any conventional form of observance. It will be interesting to mark the features of the celebrations held on this first occurrence of the day ; and they may prove useful in suggesting forms of celebration for future years.

The initial observance of the day, on the scene of the important events of the original and unproclaimed "Patriots' Day," was ushered in by a meeting on the evening of the 18th of April at the Old North Church

(Christ Church) in Salem Street, Boston, which was at once a congratulatory occasion celebrating the restoration to a condition of use of its ancient and excellent chimes, and a commemoration of the hanging in the tower of the church the two signal lanterns which informed Paul Revere, the chief herald of Revolutionary events, of the route the troops were taking. Seated in or near the chancel were the governor and other State dignitaries, with quite a number of the leading clergymen and citizens of Boston, several of whom addressed the meeting. The Rev. Dr. S. F. Smith, author of "America," presented a new poem,[1] relating to the signal lanterns and the messenger. The most striking, as well as the most pleasing, feature of the evening to the outside congregation occurred at the close of the exercises in the audience room, when two lanterns were carried through the church to the belfry by the sexton, who was followed by the members of the Old Colony Guild of Bell Ringers (of tower chimes). The lanterns were hung from the same window as in 1775; and then the peals from the chimes began, rolling their impressive, suggestive, and delightful melody over the north end of the city and to the shores across the Charles and the inner harbor.

The signal was observed, as of yore, and a waiting horseman then imitated the galloping ride of Paul Revere; and his shouts of alarm were as numerously heard, if not as terrifying, as those of the Revolutionary messenger.

CONCORD.

But Concord and Lexington certainly should be points of chief attention. The programme of Con-

---

[1] Given among the poems of the day in this volume.

cord's celebration was carried out as follows: The red, white, and blue floated from every available point; and bunting greeted the eye on every hand, especially in the historic localities. At sunrise the bells were rung, and the Concord Independent Battery fired a salute of fifty guns from the hill overlooking the village. At noon a salute of nineteen guns was fired, and the bells rung. At six o'clock the final salute of fifty guns was given, while the bells again pealed out. There was band music at intervals at various points through the day, a formal concert being given on Monument Square at one o'clock. Other events of the day were a military parade by the third battalion of the sixth regiment at 8.45 A.M.; the sham fight between a body of militia representing the Provincials and a large company of colored soldiers representing the British; another general parade at 2 P.M., culminating in a reception to the governor and other distinguished guests; at 12 M. the Massachusetts Society of the Sons of the American Revolution held its sixth annual meeting, which was concluded by a dinner with speeches; and a concert and ball in the town hall completed the festivities of the day.

LEXINGTON.

From early morning until late in the afternoon, Massachusetts Avenue, leading from Boston through Cambridge and Arlington to the historic centres of Lexington and Concord, the route of the British troops one hundred and nineteen years before, was crowded with pleasure vehicles of all sorts, equestrians, pedestrians, and bicycles. Public buildings, business blocks, and many dwellings were decorated, and flags and colored draperies were plentiful. The celebration in

Lexington began early in the morning, when the Lexington drum-corps and the color-guard of the public schools marched over the route taken by the " redcoats " on that most memorable 19th of April, and awaked the *fin de siècle* inhabitants from their peaceful slumbers.   At ten o'clock the governor and his party arrived by the railway, and were met at the station by a division from the Grand Army, and a detachment from the Naval Brigade, — the line proceeding to the Common, — the old Lexington Green.   Here all who could, of the procession and people, entered the Hancock Church, where music and addresses were in course ; while the overflow of people was entertained by an out-door band concert, the latter being repeated at intervals through the day.   A light lunch was served to the guests at the Old Belfry Club House, followed by a drive in the suburbs ; afterward they, with a large number of others, enjoyed a banquet and speeches in the Town Hall.   There were also several private entertainments during the day.   The celebration closed with a grand civic ball.

BOSTON.

At sunrise bells were rung, and flags were displayed on all city buildings and on the public staffs.   There were also many private flags flying.   At 10 A.M. dedicatory exercises were held in the new Agassiz schoolhouse in Jamaica Plain.   At 10.30 commenced a twelve-oared barge race for amateurs on Charles River, three hundred dollars in trophies being given as prizes.   At 12 M. there was a salute of one hundred guns fired on the Common by a battery of artillery, together with ringing of bells.   From 3.30 to 5.30 P.M. there was a band concert on the Common.   At sunset the bells were rung again, ending the municipal celebration. Many organizations observed the day, among which were the Daughters of the American Revolution (Old South Meeting-house), Tenth Mass. Battery Association (sixteenth annual reunion and dinner), Second Light Battery Association (annual reunion and dinner), King's Daughters and Sons (oratorical and literary entertainment for the benefit of their ·State headquarters), Ladies' Aid Society (festival in aid of St. Mary's Infant Asylum), and others. There were also many private entertainments during day and evening.

In Worcester the first observance of Patriots' Day began at midnight, when a Paul Revere, in Colonial costume, on a white horse, rode through many of the streets on the west side of the city, awakening the residents with pistol-shots and calls to arms. Through the day and evening there were many entertainments and celebrations of various kinds by organizations and private persons.

In Salem Patriots' Day was celebrated in a moderate way. All of the church-bells were rung at morning, noon, and evening, and salutes were fired. Entertainments were given in all of the principal halls, and several dances were held.

In Lowell business was generally suspended. The national colors were displayed on all public buildings, Grand Army halls, public and parochial schools, and upon the flagstaffs on the commons. Exercises were held by various organizations.

Fitchburg had slight local observance, its military organizations passing the day at Concord.

In Lynn Patriots' Day was quietly observed. Business was largely suspended, the factories and stores being closed, and people went in numbers to Concord and Lexington.

In Dedham Patriots' Day was a great day, and only when its two hundred and fiftieth anniversary was observed has it witnessed so successful a celebration of any one day or occasion.

In Peabody the old Lexington monument, where the minute-men assembled at the summons of Gideon Foster, was decorated in honor of the new holiday.

In Sudbury the public schools held exercises commemorative of the day.

The Beverly Historical Society celebrated Patriots' Day in an appropriate manner, which included addresses and an oration.

At Bedford a company of children with cornet and drums turned out and marched to the old village burial-ground, where they rendered selections of national airs, while the town's committee placed flags on the graves of those who participated in the experiences of one hundred and nineteen years ago.

From Lawrence, twenty miles from Concord, a long cavalcade traversed the route of the British, attended by a band of music, also mounted.

At Cambridge the public schools were closed, and all the public buildings and many private ones were decorated. The Lafayette Club, composed of French-Americans, held a patriotic public meeting, which was largely attended.

In Waltham Patriots' Day was observed in a quiet manner. Business was almost entirely suspended, and hundreds went to Lexington and Concord. The Emmet Literary Association presented *Arrah na Pogue* at the Park Theatre afternoon and evening.

In Arlington there was a meeting of the Improvement Association in the Town Hall in the evening, which was addressed by leading citizens.

In Acton business was suspended, and nearly all

the inhabitants joined with Concord in its celebration. But the bells were rung at morning, noon, and night, and there was an entertainment at the Town Hall in the evening.

In the town of Wellesley the day was not greatly observed. In the evening, however, the members of the college community (Wellesley College — female), with a few invited guests, assembled in the chapel for the appointed special service. After an organ prelude, Prof. Margaret E. Stratton read the governor's proclamation of "Patriots' Day," and the Beethoven Club sang *The Star-spangled Banner*, the audience joining in the chorus. The venerable Rev. Dr. Webb offered prayer, which was followed by an address from Rev. Edward G. Porter, D.D., of Lexington ; who, by the aid of a chart, gave an account of the country from Boston to Lexington, and of the principal events which occurred at different points. At the close of the address the audience sang *America*, and a benediction then closed the observance.

The foregoing accounts embrace all the varieties in celebration (not all the celebrations) which have come to notice. Formerly, in the interior towns, the observances of Fast Day were generally religious meetings and ball-games, with here and there public and private dances ; and Patriots' Day merely had fewer of the meetings and more ball-playing. Bicycles, a recent feature of the country roads, were more numerous than ever before, and in some localities were quite impressive in their processions and evolutions.

OBSERVANCE BY SOCIAL ORGANIZATIONS OF
PATRIOTS' DAY

THE Massachusetts Society of the Sons of the American Revolution, at noon of the 19th, held a reunion in the First Parish Church in Concord, where the first Provincial Congress was held. It was voted to petition the Boston city government to mark the graves of Revolutionary soldiers, sailors, and patriots in that city, the number of graves being estimated at scarcely more than one hundred. It was thought this might be accomplished before another recurrence of this holiday. Some routine business was transacted; and the society and its guests, to the number of about three hundred, then enjoyed a dinner in the vestry, enlivened by speeches from persons eminent in the State and Nation.

The Ohio Society of the Sons of the American Revolution celebrated the battles of Lexington and Concord at Columbus, Ohio, on the evening of the 19th of April. Governor McKinley spoke to the toast, "Ohio, an empire founded by the heroes of the American Revolution." There were several other speeches by eminent men.

The Daughters of the Revolution, Massachusetts chapter, met, on the afternoon of Patriots' Day, at Ruby Parlors, 62 Beacon Street. Mrs. William Lee, the State regent, who presided, made an address and related the history of the association, paying tribute to Mrs. Jane G. Austen, the novelist, a member recently deceased. A paper upon the life and deeds of Paul Revere was read by Elbridge H. Goss, his biographer; Rev. Dr. Edward Everett Hale spoke about the hymn *America;* and Miss Charlotte W. Hawes spoke about the chime bells of Christ Church. Refreshments and a social reception followed, closing the occasion.

THE DAUGHTERS OF THE AMERICAN REVOLUTION.

A new chapter of this organization was formed on April 15, in Boston, and adopted the name " Paul Revere." This chapter, with visiting members of the society from other States, attended the meeting held by the Warren and Prescott chapters at the Old South Meeting-house, at 11.30 A. M., on Patriots' Day, to commemorate the deeds of April 19, 1775. Samuel Eliot, LL.D., presided. There were orchestral and vocal music, and addresses by the president of the day, by Prof. Edward Channing of Harvard University, and Dr. Edward Everett Hale. These were followed by the reading of an original poem, entitled *Our Country,* by Mrs. Julia Ward Howe; and Rev. Dr. S. F. Smith told, in a very interesting way, of how *America* was written.

In New York City the day was appropriately celebrated by the city chapter of the Daughters of the American Revolution, the meeting being held in the old Fraunce Tavern, at the corner of Broad and Pearl streets, where General Washington gathered his generals on the day in which the British evacuated the city. The tavern was profusely decorated with American flags, palms, and lilies. The occasion included the reading of an address by Mrs. Schuyler Hamilton, of a poem by Miss Clinton Jones, and patriotic songs. It was the third anniversary of this chapter. On the same day the general society of the Daughters met at a luncheon in the gold-and-white ballroom of the Waldorf, in celebration of the battle of Lexington. One hundred patriotic women were ranged about a horseshoe table, and beside each plate was a bouquet of daffodils tied with blue ribbon.

The Colonial Society of Massachusetts held its April meeting on Patriots' Day, in the hall of the American Academy of Arts and Sciences. The principal feature of the occasion was the address of Dr. Edward G. Porter on the affair at Lexington and Concord, who confined his treatment to the happenings between Lexington Green and Concord Bridge, which he related in minute detail. In the afternoon a Colonial party was given at Hendrie Hall, Dorchester. The halls were lavishly decorated with laurel, palms, and flowers, while the two balconies were effectively draped with large flags. The invitations were etched on parchment, the upper right-hand corner bearing a sketch of the figure of a "minuteman." The document was sealed and tied with the national colors. The orders were little American flags with the programme attached. The assembly danced until the sun had set. The affair was pronounced a grand success.

THE KING'S DAUGHTERS,

on the afternoon of the 19th, gave a patriotic entertainment at the People's Church, in Boston, for the benefit of the State headquarters of the International Order of the King's Daughters and Sons. The broad platform was appropriately decorated with flags, and with the oil portraits of General Washington and his wife. On the platform were Rev. Drs. Edward

Everett Hale and S. F. Smith, Julia Ward Howe, Miss Charlotte Hawes, and Miss Gertrude E. Smith, who each took part in the exercises, — Dr. Smith reading a new hymn,[1] written for the occasion. Two young ladies, Misses Whittier and Stephen, added greatly to the entertainment by their delightful singing. The presiding genius of the day was Mrs. Charlotte S. Doolittle, who stands at the head of the twenty thousand King's Daughters in Massachusetts.

THE DAUGHTERS OF VERMONT,

resident in Boston and vicinity, held a reception in the state apartments at the Hotel Vendome on the eve of Patriots' Day, which was attended by many New England ladies and gentlemen of eminence.

In a rear apartment refreshments were served by groups of fair young girls, either daughters or granddaughters of Vermont. The Symphony Mandolin and Guitar Club rendered a light music that proved very suitable and delightful.

[1] This hymn opens the poetical portion of this volume.

THE ANCIENT AND HONORABLE ARTILLERY COMPANY

was already "ancient" when the battles of Lexington and Concord became incidents of history; and it was quite fitting that its members should observe Patriots' Day. This they did, to the number of a hundred and fifty, by a banquet at the Quincy House, a band playing national and patriotic airs in the intervals between the speeches.

The annual reunion and thirtieth anniversary of the Second Light Battery Association, which includes Battery B, M.V.M., and Company A, Forty-second Massachusetts Volunteers, was held in the Crawford House on the 19th.

The sixteenth annual reunion and dinner of the Tenth Massachusetts Light Battery Association took place at the American House in the afternoon, about fifty comrades participating.

Company A, Ninth Infantry, Captain Keefe, observed Patriots' Day by partaking of its annual dinner in the evening in the American House.

168

BENEVOLENT AND RELIGIOUS ASSOCIATIONS.

SEVERAL benevolent associations in Boston and neighboring places held receptions and entertainments for their institutions and patrons, in some cases successfully seeking pecuniary aid. The most notable and extensive of these, whose report has come to hand, was that of St. Mary's Infant Asylum, held at the East Armory, Boston. There were a large number of tables with articles for sale; and for entertainment, there were, in the afternoon, social dancing, with orchestral music, also scarf and other spectacular dances, and songs by little girls; in the evening, Spanish dances by eight little girls, and by professionals from the new Bijou Theatre, interspersed with superior vocal music.

The parishioners of St. Augustine's Church (Roman Catholic), in South Boston, celebrated the day in a quiet and patriotic manner, listening to national songs rendered by the St. Augustine Glee Club, assisted by a chorus of two hundred children dressed in red, white, and blue, and to a lecture by Hon. Thomas J. Gargan on "The Obligations of Catholics as Citizens of the Republic." In his peroration the orator said :—

"We may not be called upon to make sacrifices upon the field of battle like the men of the Revolution, or the men who fought to keep the Union whole; yet every generation must fight the battle for the right; we must preserve the patrimony that came to us from our ancestors, and transmit it unimpaired to succeeding generations, to the end that the dignity, the credit, and the honor of this government of the people may be maintained."

BIBLIOGRAPHY

OF THE

NINETEENTH OF APRIL, 1775.

BANCROFT'S *History of the United States.*

HILDRETH'S *History of the United States.*

ELLIOTT'S *History of New England.*

PALFREY'S *History of New England.*

ADAMS'S *History of New England.*

AUSTIN'S *History of Massachusetts.* Illustrated.

VARNEY'S *Gazetteer of Massachusetts.* Illustrated.

SHATTUCK'S *History of Concord, Mass.* Illustrated.

HUDSON'S *History of Lexington, Mass.* Illustrated.

FROTHINGHAM'S *Siege of Boston,* 1849–1873. Illustrated.

GOSS's *Life of Col. Paul Revere.* 1891. Many illustrations.

EDWARD EVERETT'S *Mount Vernon Papers.*

EDWARD E. HALE'S *One Hundred Years Ago.*

LOSSING'S *Field-Book of the Revolution.* Illustrated.

DRAKE'S *History of Middlesex County.* Illustrated.

DRAKE'S *Historic Scenes and Mansions of Middlesex County.* Illustrated.

HOWELLS's *Three Villages.*

BARTLETT'S *Concord Guide-Book.* 1887. Illustrated.

Handbook of Lexington. Boston, 1891. Illustrated.

Souvenir of 1775. By REV. EDWARD G. PORTER and H. M. STEVENSON. 1875. Illustrated.

Cooper's "Lionel Lincoln" has a vivid account of the day as a setting for certain characters in that novel.

For a more thorough investigation, consult in addition the histories of Cambridge, Somerville, Arlington, Lincoln, Bedford, Acton, and Sudbury; also "The Reader's Handbook of the Revolution," by Justin Winsor (Boston, 1880), and "The Nineteenth of April in Literature," by James L. Whitney (Concord, Mass., 1876). The last two volumes mention pamphlets, magazine articles, and manuscripts, as well as books.